MURDER ON TOUR

A HUGH RENNERT MYSTERY

MURDER ON TOUR

A HUGH RENNERT MYSTERY

Todd Downing

Coachwhip Publications

Greenville, Ohio

Murder on Tour by Todd Downing
Copyright © 2013 Estate of Todd Downing
First published 1933, copyright renewed.
Permission to reprint granted by the Estate of Todd Downing.
Introduction © 2013 Curtis Evans

ISBN 1-61646-170-5
ISBN-13 978-1-61646-170-6

Cover Image: Mictlantecuhtli © Vladimir Korostyshevskiy

CoachwhipBooks.com

CONTENTS

Part Three: Mexico City—Laredo

INTRODUCTION
DAY OF THE DEAD: TODD DOWNING AND *MURDER ON TOUR*
CURTIS EVANS

BORN OF PARTLY Indigenous American parentage in 1902 in the small city of Atoka, Choctaw Nation, Indian Territory (later Oklahoma), Todd Downing while in college at the University of Oklahoma in the 1920s developed two consuming intellectual interests: Mexico and mystery fiction. In 1933, these two interests happily converged in Downing's first published book, *Murder on Tour*, a detective novel set primarily in Mexico City. After eight decades *Murder on Tour* is back in print, under the auspices of Coachwhip Publications.

From the University of Oklahoma Todd Downing received a B.A. in 1924 and an M.A. in 1928. Additionally, in 1925 the OU languages department hired Downing as an instructor in Spanish, a position he would hold until he resigned from the university faculty ten years later, in order to devote himself fulltime to authorship. Before writing *Murder on Tour*, Downing took classes at the *Universidad Nacional Autónoma de Mexico* (National Autonomous University of Mexico) and conducted tourist parties in Mexico City and the surrounding area. This experience not unnaturally found its way into *Murder on Tour*, which Downing probably wrote mostly in Mexico City, during June and July 1932. (He likely made any finishing touches in August, after he returned to Oklahoma.) The manuscript was accepted by G. P. Putnam's Sons in May 1933 and published in September. (For biographical detail on Todd Downing, see my 2013 book, published by Coachwhip Publications, *Clues and Corpses: The Detective Fiction and Mystery Criticism of Todd Downing.*)

While he was writing *Murder on Tour* during the summer of 1932, Downing read two Ellery Queen detective novels, both of which he reviewed for the Oklahoma City *Daily Oklahoman*. (Downing reviewed nearly 300 mystery novels and short story collections for the *Daily Oklahoman* between 1930 and 1937.) Downing's reviews of this pair of Queens, *The Dutch Shoe Mystery* and *The Greek Coffin Mystery*, give us clues to the aesthetic values the Oklahoma author held at the time he wrote *Murder on Tour*. Of *The Dutch Shoe Mystery* a delighted Downing enthused: "If your brain needs exercise buy, borrow or steal a copy of this book." He predicted that "if the public knows good detective stories when it reads them" Ellery Queen would soon enjoy the "phenomenal success" of bestselling detective novelist S. S. Van Dine, creator of the gentleman amateur detective Philo Vance.[1]

With its plot centering on a carefully constructed and fairly clued murder puzzle, *Murder on Tour* reflects Todd Downing's deep immersion in the classical, "fair play" detective fiction that captured the eager interest of many intelligent readers during the mystery genre's Golden Age (roughly 1920 to 1939). In addition to the criminous work of Ellery Queen, Downing at this time also avidly read the mystery fiction of the future Queen of Crime, Agatha Christie. In a 1931 *Daily Oklahoman* review, Downing lauded Christie's first Miss Marple mystery, *The Murder at the Vicarage*, declaring that "readers who like to match wits with the author in the solution of baffling mysteries should not fail to read Miss Christie's latest novel."[2] In 1931 Downing praised in print as well the plotting skills of such now faded mystery lights as Anthony Abbot, Anthony Wynne, H. C. Bailey, and Charles J. Dutton.

Conversely, Downing faulted detective novels, like Madeleine Sharps' *The Black Pearl Murders* (1931), that failed to offer readers

---

[1] Evans, *Clues and Corpses: The Detective Fiction and Mystery Criticism of Todd Downing* (Coachwhip, 2013), 176. Downing's mystery book reviews are collected in *Clues and Corpses*, as is his 1943 essay on crime fiction, "Murder Is a Rather Serious Business."

[2] Evans, *Clues and Corpses*, 154-155.

much in the way of plotting ingenuity and fair play. (Sharps' novel "could have been better improved . . . by adding a more reasonable solution," Downing sniffed.) In a 1931 review of the detective novel *Murder in Four Degrees*, authored by the popular though routine English writer J. S. Fletcher, Downing resignedly speculated that "mystery fans who like to rack their brains over problems in deduction are in a minority compared with those who read to pass the time away."[3]

Murder on Tour did not then—and will not now—appeal to tired readers desiring merely some sort of bedtime soporific. Those who like to put their minds to work on a challenging fictional murder problem, however, will find one in the pages that follow. Not for nothing did the great English crime fiction critic and crossword puzzle deviser Edward Powys Mathers ("Torquemada") pronounce that "Mr. Downing is a born detective story writer."[4]

Yet *Murder on Tour* also offers readers additional pleasures besides a teasing puzzle. To be sure, Downing loved a good baffler, but he also valued tales of crime and detection that were stylishly written, convincingly characterized and viscerally exciting. One of the strongest reviews Downing gave a book in 1931 was for George A. Birmingham's *The Hymn Tune Mystery*, primarily on account of the novel's "well-drawn characters." Downing urged "those superior persons who scorn mystery stories . . . to read this one." Similarly, Downing in 1931 praised Anthony Abbot's *About the Murder of Geraldine Foster* and Anthony Wynne's *The Silver Scale Mystery* (*Murder of a Lady*) not only for their puzzles, but for their thrills. "What makes the story remain in the memory of the reader is the element of horror which permeates the tale," Downing avowed of *About the Murder of Geraldine Foster*.[5]

In terms of purely literary qualities, *Murder on Tour* is distinguished most by its Mexico City setting, so familiar to Downing after his four Mexican summers. Following a terse prologue set in

[3] Ibid., 172-173.

[4] *London Observer*, 19 January 1936, 6.

[5] Evans, *Clues and Corpses*, 157, 161.

a hotel in San Antonio, where a sudden, savage slaying occurs, *Murder on Tour* is divided into three parts: a short opening section also set in San Antonio; a long middle section set in Mexico City; and a lengthy closing section that takes place on a train traveling from Mexico City to Laredo. The murdered man, a young United States Treasury Department customs agent investigating the smuggling by Americans of Mexican antiquities, was strangled in his San Antonio hotel room with a black silk stocking. (His manner of death was perhaps suggested to Downing by *The Silk Stocking Murders*, a 1920s Anthony Berkeley detective novel that he owned.) With official suspicion centering on the thirteen members of the Inter-American Tours party about to set forth from San Antonio to Mexico City, senior customs agent Hugh Rennert joins the party to catch a killer. (Rennert would serve as Downing's series detective for a total of seven novels and one novella.)

In his first fictional appearance Hugh Rennert is described as "having rather homely but not undistinguished features—thin, dark brown hair brushed back from a high forehead and clear brown eyes, flecked with gray." The set of Rennert's "firm square chin" offsets "a certain almost dreamy look" in his eyes. He is a dreamer then, but also a doer. Elsewhere in the novel Downing describes Rennert in decidedly demystified terms simply as a "middle-aged man with gray hair beginning to show at the temples."[6] Downing is careful to present his detective as a regular man, rather than an eccentric, quotation-spouting genius with a collection of esoteric bric-a-brac or a hard-boiled tough guy adept at boozing, bedding, and brawling.

Hugh Rennert's suspects in the tour party are efficiently sketched, easily distinguishable American "types" doubtlessly familiar to Downing from his personal experience as a tour guide. He brightly satirizes some of these types, including Miss Tredkin, the puritanical temperance crusader from Wichita, Kansas ("When I see men, American men, down here in Mexico, reeling in the streets and through hotel lobbies under the influence of drink,

---

[6] Todd Downing, *Murder on Tour*, 25, 42.

forgetful of their manhood and of the ties which bind them to their loved ones at home, I say 'Thank God for Kansas!'") and Dr. Bymaster, a Colorado university professor who is the first in a long line of fictional American "experts" on Mexico at whom Downing in his novels casts a more than mildly sardonic eye ("[My book] is to be an economic survey of our modern world, with especial emphasis on the undeveloped resources in backward countries, such as Mexico"). All the members of the tour party have some quality that raises the suspicions of Hugh Rennert—and those of the reader.

Downing touches on local highlights of Mexico City and the surrounding area, such as Chapultepec Castle, Lake Xochimilco and Sanborns department store, but by far the most notable Mexican element that he develops in *Murder on Tour* is the *Dia de los Muertos* (Day of the Dead), which takes place in the novel. Indeed, *Day of the Dead* might well have served as an alternate title for *Murder on Tour*. This macabre Mexican national holiday in honor of the dead—who, it is said, walk among the living at this time— has its origins in beliefs of Indigenous Americans, which invariably fascinated Downing.

Like his creator, Hugh Rennert is powerfully drawn to *vacilada*, the stoically mirthful Mexican attitude to death. As he grasps a toy skeleton purchased by a member of the tour party, Rennert ruminates on his deep longing to truly absorb the native temperament:

> Rennert, fingering idly the painted toy, felt stealing over him a curious relaxation of the senses and, at the same time, was vaguely aware of tension. . . . His finger released the spring at the base of the toy. Instantly the little skeleton jumped into life, began his macabre dance. The left hand jerked the bottle to his lips, the right hand fell to his side. The right hand waggishly thumbed a nose, the left hand fell to his side. The roguish eyes looked into Rennert's.
>
> A boon companion, he mused, with an invitation. *Memento mori.* There flashed across his memory a

steel engraving (Was it by Doré?) in an old book which as a boy he had found in the attic. A grim, frightful old man with a long white beard. In one hand he held a scythe, its edge curved like his nose. With the other he beckoned inexorably. Rennert remembered waking in the middle of the night bathed in cold sweat while he stared into the darkness at the foot of the bed, where the old man had been standing. Yet the next day, with perverse eagerness, he had stolen up the attic stairs, and gazed again at the picture.[7]

Downing's Day of the Dead theme is linked in a moving way with the person who arguably is the most interesting character in the novel, the dignified widow Mrs. Priscilla Evans Rankin, a "fragile little woman with pearl gray hair and a quietly beautiful face" who returns every year to Mexico.[8] Moreover, the Day of the Dead theme underscores the constant menace facing the members of the tour party. Death lurks among these people, literally as well as figuratively.

As mentioned above, Rennert becomes involved in this murder case because of his investigation, in his capacity as a customs service agent, of American thefts of Mexican antiquities. Downing himself had a small collection of Mexican artifacts (see illustrations), but he was outraged by American pilfering, which he saw as another form of colonialist exploitation of Mexico by the United States. In *Murder on Tour* Hugh Rennert clearly speaks for his creator on this subject. "Since the Revolution," lectures the customs service agent, "the Mexican government has awakened to the fact that they are letting foreigners take out of the country most of their great archaeological treasures." Rennert specifically references the highhanded, controversial actions of a former U. S. consul in Mexico, Edward Herbert Thompson, who from 1904 to 1910

[7] Downing, *Tour*, 66.

[8] Ibid., 50.

An artifact in Todd Downing's collection.

Artifacts in Todd Downing's collection.

dredged the sacred well (*cenote*) at the Mexican archaeological site of Chichen Itza and sent the relics he discovered out of the country to the Peabody Museum of Natural History at Yale University.[9] In its handling of this delicate subject matter, *Murder on Tour* shares affinity with *A Thief of Time*, a celebrated 1988 detective novel by another Oklahoma crime writer, the late Tony Hillerman.

Murder on Tour is a sterling example of the kind of mystery that Todd Downing himself most enjoyed reading: a clever fair play puzzle embellished with a lively narrative, some interesting characters and a fascinating setting. Todd Downing would take Hugh Rennert back to Mexico in six more intriguing detective novels— *The Cat Screams* (1934), *Vultures in the Sky* (1935), *Murder on the Tropic* (1935), *The Case of the Unconquered Sisters* (1936), *The Last Trumpet* (1937), and *Night over Mexico* (1937)—before retiring him in favor of a newer character, Rennert's friend Texas sheriff Peter Bounty. First appearing in *The Last Trumpet*, Bounty would serve as the detective in two Downing novels, *Death under the Moonflower* (1938), and *The Lazy Lawrence Murders* (1941). Additionally, Downing published an acclaimed non-fictional study of Mexico, *The Mexican Earth*, in 1940. He also started writing an ambitious historical novel about Mexico, *Under the Rose*, but although the novel was slated to be published in 1942 it never appeared in print and apparently no copy of it in any form survives today.

Downing in fact published no additional novels of any sort after 1941. However, a Hugh Rennert novella, *The Shadowless Hour*, almost certainly originally written in 1931 or 1932, was published in periodical form in 1945 in *Mystery Book Magazine*. Cannibalized by Downing for use in *The Cat Screams*, *Vultures in the Sky* and *Murder on the Tropic*, *The Shadowless Hour* has elements of interest, though more for the scholar or completist than the general reader.

His career as a novelist gone defunct by the early 1940s, Todd Downing left Oklahoma in 1942 and moved to Philadelphia, where he found employment as an advertising copy writer with the prominent firm of N. W. Ayer & Son. Downing's creative impetus remained

[9] Ibid., 161.

with him, even in this environment. One of his advertisements, commissioned by the Electric Light & Power Association, was a tongue-in-cheek mystery homage featuring that icon of Golden Age detective fiction, a keyed house plan. This witty print advertisement, titled "The Case of the Crumpled Letter," was later honored with inclusion in Julius Lewis Watkins' *The 100 Greatest Advertisements* (Dover, 1959).

In the first half of the 1950s Downing left the advertising business to teach at schools in Maryland and Virginia, before finally moving back for good to his hometown Atoka to reside with his widowed mother, now in her eighties. For some dozen years Downing taught Spanish and French at Atoka High School, from where he had graduated back in 1920. Late in his life, he was honored with an emeritus professorship of Choctaw Language and Choctaw Heritage at Southeastern Oklahoma State University (then Southeastern State College) in nearby Durant, Oklahoma; and he played a significant role in developing the college's nascent bilingual education program.

Standing 5'6", Todd Downing was a trim, fastidious and formal man who made a habit of always wearing a coat and tie. At some point, probably in the 1950s, he left the Presbyterian faith in which he had been raised and became a Quaker. He embraced pacifism and in the 1960s was a vocal critic of the Vietnam War. By the 1960s Downing seems as well to have lost his interest of many years' standing in mystery fiction. Rather than reading tales of fictional murder, Downing in his spare time perused gardening books and tended the plants around his old family home in Atoka, where he lived alone after the death of his mother in 1965. He also became a great devotee of classical music, particularly opera.[10]

Forty years and four months after the publication of *Murder on Tour*, Todd Downing died from a pulmonary embolism on January 9,

---

[10] Nenad Downing to the author, 21, 22 January 2013. Nenad Downing is the son of Todd Downing's sister, Ruth Shields Downing. This information in the following two paragraphs as well is drawn from my correspondence with Nenad Downing.

1974, at the age of 71 (a longtime heavy smoker, he also was afflicted with terminal emphysema). Before his death Downing was hopefully planning the composition of a final work, a history of the Choctaw people, and in pursuit of this cherished project he had recently completed a research trip to Mississippi. Yet Death had different plans for Downing, and took him to another destination.

At Todd Downing's funeral in Atoka, four Choctaws in native dress danced and chanted around his coffin, before it was finally lowered into the ground.

Memento mori.

GERMANTOWN, TENNESSEE
FEBRUARY 2013

PROLOGUE
NIGHT IN SAN ANTONIO

THE PAST LIES HEAVILY upon San Antonio. Despite the skyscrapers, the clanging street cars, it is there—a residue of past glories, making itself known in the faint acrid odor of decay arising from crumbling, bullet-pocked 'dobe walls, in the memories of spilt blood that, one feels, still lurk somewhere behind the dark eyes of the descendants of the people who named her. Like a spearhead—this city and these people—thrust from the dark mass below the Rio Grande toward the vitals of a white-skinned, machine-making land. A spearhead. . . .

A young man stood at the window of a San Antonio hotel room, gazing out over the dormant city, letting the soft night air flood over his closed eyelids.

He felt curiously exhilarated, like a swimmer who senses that he is nearing a yet unseen goal. Exhilarated and yet vaguely uneasy, conscious of a treacherous undertow beneath glass-smooth water.

He yawned, turned into the darkened room and crawled between the cool sheets. The springs of the bed creaked slightly as he stretched his long limbs.

When he awoke it was the stillness of the room that impressed his sharply awakened senses. The room was very still.

It came again—a light rap upon the panel of his door. He reached over and switched on the lamp beside the bed. Slipping on his dressing gown, he arose and went to the door, opened it.

He stared for a second in utter surprise at the person who stood there.

"Why," he faltered, "good evening. Won't you come in?"

The other smiled pleasantly but did not speak until the door was closed and they stood in the room together. An odd little laugh punctuated the words:

"Sorry to disturb you, Mr.—ah—Payne, but I wanted very much to talk to you—before we leave for Mexico in the morning."

Mexico. Payne was suddenly alert. With one hand he gestured toward a chair, while with the other he drew the dressing gown more closely about him.

"No," the other said softly, "let's stand by the window. It is close in here and the night is lovely."

They walked to the window and stood there, gazing out into the star-drenched night. A vague uneasiness crept over Payne. *A sordid business*, he thought, *like that upon which I'm engaged.* Out over the airport a thin pencil of light sliced the darkness. The city was very still, so still that he almost imagined that he heard the gentle closing of a door. *Or else*, the thought stabbed, *a trap, an old, old trap. . . .*

His hands flew upward to throw away the soft, constricting thing about his throat. He felt himself borne quickly backward. . . .

PART ONE
TEXAS

San Antonio	Lv.	9:45 A.M.
Laredo	Ar.	2:45 P.M.

1
THE PRESS

(FROM THE SAN ANTONIO *EVENING TRANSCRIPT* OF OCT. 27, 1933)

SILK STOCKINGS USED
TO STRANGLE MAN
IN PATIO HOTEL MURDER
Mystery cloaks brutal slaying of visitor registered
here as John Payne of Kansas City
"DO NOT DISTURB" SIGN ON DOOR
Murder occurred about midnight;
body found by woman this morning

MYSTERY SHROUDS the strangulation of a man registered at the Patio Hotel under the name of John Payne, of Kansas City, Mo., about midnight last night in his hotel room.

The dead man, a pair of black silk stockings tightly knotted about his neck, was discovered at noon today by Miss Mamie Denzil, hotel maid, who disregarded a "Do Not Disturb" sign on the door and entered to clean the room.

"I knocked and when no one answered I used my pass key to enter," Miss Denzil said in an exclusive statement to the *Transcript*. "When I saw that a man had been strangled with a pair of silk stockings I screamed and used the house telephone to call

downstairs and notify the clerk. The window lead-
ing to the fire escape was open."

After a thorough examination of the body, Dr. G.
E. Wilkerson, county medical examiner, said that
death occurred between 11:30 and midnight, or
shortly after. Death was due to strangulation.

An overturned ash tray was the only evidence of
a struggle in the room. A key to the room was found
at the foot of the fire escape which leads from the
window.

Inspector Hayner Miles, of the city police force,
has been assigned to the case. Police are attempting
to establish the dead man's identity through contact
with officers in Kansas City.

2
ABOUT SILK STOCKINGS

"MURDER," SAID INSPECTOR MILES of the San Antonio police to the man in the blue serge suit who sat across the desk from him, "is rather out of your field, I understand that, Mr. Rennert."

"Yes," the other replied. His eyes rested for a moment on the two black silk stockings which he held in his hand and he added under his breath: "Thank God!"

The inspector, himself a tall, red-faced man who found his blue uniform a trifle tight about the neck and the waist, gazed speculatively at the mild, even-voiced man.

This man had rather homely but not undistinguished features—thin, dark brown hair brushed back from a high forehead and clear brown eyes, flecked with gray. Probably a pleasant fellow to know, Inspector Miles decided. He liked the set of that firm square chin. It offset a certain almost dreamy look in those eyes. Still, when it came to a murder case . . .

"You've been to the hotel?" he asked.

"Yes. Sergeant Watts showed me over the place."

"You think our theory about the murder is correct?"

"I feel sure it is. Every precaution was taken to prevent discovery of the body before the party left day before yesterday morning."

"We will, of course, continue the investigation at this end, and keep you informed as to anything that turns up."

"I shall be anxious to learn if you find out where and by whom these stockings were bought." He laid them carefully upon the desk and gazed at them thoughtfully.

"I've got men working on that angle now. It ought to be easy to find out if they were bought in San Antonio."

Rennert picked up his soft gray hat and ran a finger down the crease in the top. He looked up suddenly, a frown on his face.

"Are you married, Inspector?"

"Married? Why, yes. Why?"

"Then you ought to know something about silk stockings."

Inspector Miles settled back uneasily in his chair. This Rennert fellow, he decided, was rather unpredictable. He hoped he wouldn't feel called upon to make any of the obvious, intimate references. The inspector was nearing the retirement age and was beginning to indulge in sentimental expectations of a little home out in the country. He had long since lost his taste for the cruder sexual jokes.

He decided to be noncommittal. "I pay for them," he said.

He glanced at his watch, just as a reminder to this fellow that his office was a place of business. "Your train leaves at 9: 45, doesn't it?" he asked.

The other man's eyes were on a fleecy white cloud sailing slowly across the patch of blue sky framed by the open window. There was an amused twinkle in those eyes.

"I was referring," he said, "to the color."

"The color?"

"Yes." The twinkle died out of Rennert's eyes and he leaned forward in his chair. "Does your wife have a pair of black silk stockings?" he demanded. "Black?"

"Why, I don't know. I can't say I ever noticed the color particularly." What the devil was this fellow driving at?

"Probably not. No woman, with any regard for style, wears black stockings any more." He nodded toward the top of the desk. "Those stockings are black."

Inspector Miles sat up suddenly. His respect for this Rennert went up a notch.

"I do not believe that a woman bought those stockings," Rennert continued. "If they were bought for actual wear, I am sure she did not. If they were bought for the purpose of strangling Payne, I doubt whether a woman made the purchase. Let's imagine a woman going into a store and asking for a pair of silk stockings. Even if she does not intend to wear them she will name the size and color to which she is accustomed. And it will not be black. If it is a man, the clerk will ask him for the size and color. He will name the first thing that comes into his mind. It will be, I am satisfied, black."

Their eyes met. "You think, then," Inspector Miles asked, "that a man bought those stockings for the purpose of strangling that fellow?"

"Yes," Rennert's voice hardened, "murderers have used them before. No easily procurable means for strangulation is better than silk stockings. The ordinary murderer does not carry ropes about his person. In this instance, it may have been intended to serve another purpose—"

"To throw suspicion on a woman?"

"Yes."

The inspector drummed a speculative finger upon the desktop.

"Maybe," he suggested, "a woman was clever enough to foresee that reasoning."

Rennert stood up. "Maybe," he agreed. "I shall be interested in finding out whether there is such an intelligent woman in this party."

He extended his hand. "Good-by, Inspector."

"Good-by, Rennert." Miles' hand closed about the other's. "And good luck. Keep in touch with me and," his kindly face grew serious, "let me know when you come back across the border. I'll be there—with handcuffs."

3
THE SUN-BAKED SAND

LAREDO, TEXAS, OCTOBER 29

THE SOUTHBOUND TRAIN paused beside the weather-beaten Laredo station, as if gathering energy for its passage through the long miles of cactus and mesquite-filled desert which lay beyond the meandering trickle of water boasting the proud name of Rio Grande.

Rennert swung lightly to the platform, his eyes momentarily dazzled by the afternoon sun.

A tall, spare man dressed in shirt and trousers of olive drab, who had been standing with one foot propped against the side of the station, approached him. They shook hands and walked toward the end of the platform.

"I got your message," said the man in olive drab. "Sorry to hear about Payne."

One hand fingered the close-cropped mustache whose bristles matched the red hair visible beneath the tilted-back hat. His blue eyes were on the heat-filled distance beyond the river.

"One of our best men," Rennert said. "He had spent months working on this case."

"Must have been getting close when he got bumped off?"

"Yes. He made the mistake of playing his hand alone. He was a young fellow, you know, and I understand that he wanted to get married to a girl back East. Probably thought he'd pull this off by himself and get a promotion."

They had reached the iron rail which runs along the end of the platform. Rennert rested a foot upon the rail and gazed southward to the sprawling town of Nuevo Laredo.

"You think you're on the track of his murderer?"

Rennert nodded. "Yes. In the last communication we had from Payne he said that he had gotten some information which led him to believe that the person who is at the head of this business made regular trips hack and forth across the border as a member of tourist parties. A tourist, you know, can go anywhere and do anything and not be suspected. Payne's latest information was to the effect that this person was a member of the Inter-America Tour party which crossed the border day before yesterday. He had planned to meet them in San Antonio, join the party as an ordinary tourist and try to identify this person."

"His dope must have been correct, then?"

"Yes."

"If you find out who it is, you'll try to get him extradited?"

Rennert's smile was grim. "I hope," he said, "to postpone arrest until we are back across the border. Then the Texas authorities will arrest him on a charge of murder. If there isn't proof enough to hold him for that, I lope to be able to make this other charge stick. If I find that he is getting suspicious and is not going to come back with the party, I'll have the Mexican authorities arrest him. After all, they have as much interest in this as we have. It was a protest from the Mexican government which started this investigation."

The train whistle sounded warningly and they made their way back toward the Pullman.

"I don't suppose you have run across anything new down this way?" Rennert asked.

The other man shook his head.

"No, just the usual line—a woman with half a dozen diamonds in the lining of her grip, a boatload of liquor up between here and Eagle Pass, some cocaine and marihuana down at Reynosa, but nothing that would interest you."

There was another sharp blast from the engine. Rennert extended his hand.

"Good-by, Mac."

"Good-by, Rennert—and good luck." His blue eyes met Rennert's. "And for God's sake take care of yourself. Remember what happened to Payne."

Rennert was upon the steps. His eyes were momentarily closed against the glare which rose from the bricks of the platform.

"I'll not forget Payne," he said softly, as the train moved off.

PART TWO
MEXICO CITY

4
THE FOURTEENTH TOURIST

"And so," Rennert said, "I followed your party on to Mexico City."

Dr. Lipscomb, manager of the Inter-America Tours, Inc., sat very stiff and straight in the green plush chair and looked at the black and white tie which Rennert wore.

Rennert drew out a package of cigarettes, offered one to Dr. Lipscomb and, when the latter had refused with an abstracted shake of the head, lit one.

He decided to wait a few moments before continuing. After all, one could not expect a man to maintain his equanimity when he had just been told that one so far unidentified member of the party under his supervision was a murderer, a particularly cold-blooded murderer.

He studied Lipscomb over the wavering spiral of smoke from his cigarette.

A handsome man, judged by any standards, masculine or feminine. Tall, well built and dressed in a perfectly fitting light gray suit. His dark brown hair, plastered against his head, glistened with pomade in the rather uncertain light of the single electric bulb in the ornate glass chandelier above. His mustache was a thin dark line above full red lips. His hands rested upon his knees and the tips of his long slender fingers beat gently one upon the other.

"I think, Mr. Rennert," he said slowly, "that you are mistaken. The Inter-America Tours are not open to every applicant. Every

33

person who applies for membership in them is investigated thoroughly—his standing, social and—er—financial, of course. I can assure you that the background of each one of my guests has been investigated. I cannot conceive of a person such as you mention being with us."

"Yet Payne joined your party after you had arrived in San Antonio without your suspecting his true identity."

Dr. Lipscomb frowned. "True, but his references were satisfactory. When he talked to me the day before we left, I hesitated about letting him join us. I did so only after due consideration. If I had suspected what his mission was—" He paused abruptly and his dark eyes rose to meet Rennert's. "You have not yet told me what reasons you have for thinking that one of my guests strangled him."

Rennert carefully flicked the ash from his cigarette into the tray by his side.

"The luggage tag, for one thing," he said. "A round piece of red cardboard with the words *Inter-America Tours* printed on it. It was found beneath Payne's body." He puffed slowly at his cigarette. "Might I see one of those tags?"

"Certainly." Dr. Lipscomb arose and brought a small black handbag from the closet. He put it on the floor before Rennert.

Rennert leaned over and examined carefully the round red tag which was attached to the handle by a short length of string.

"That," he said, "is exactly like the tag which was found on the floor under Payne's body, where, I believe, the murderer dropped it as he pulled the stockings from his pocket." He straightened up and with the toe of a polished black shoe toyed with the circular cardboard.

Dr. Lipscomb leaned forward quickly. "But perhaps it belonged to Mr. Payne himself? I gave him two of them when he joined the party."

Rennert shook his head, his gaze fixed on the conductor's face. "The two pieces of luggage which Payne owned were tagged," he said.

Silence fell between them. Dr. Lipscomb slowly straightened himself in his chair, as if moved by some invisible mechanism.

"How are these tags given out?" Rennert asked at length. "That is, do you yourself put them on the luggage or do you give them out to the members of your party?"

"Each guest, when he joins us, informs me how many pieces of luggage he has. I give him one of these tags for each piece. He puts them on himself."

"You didn't happen to notice whether there was any luggage which did not have a tag on the trip down, did you?"

"No, I did not. It's merely a formality, to identify my guests and to facilitate keeping all the luggage together. Many do not bother to attach the tags."

"Did you, by any chance, hand out any of these tags in San Antonio?"

Dr. Lipscomb considered. "Yes," he said deliberately, "I did. I gave Mr. Argudin and Mr. Brody one for each piece of luggage which they had. Both joined us in San Antonio. I also gave an extra one to someone else—Mr. Earp, I believe."

"Earp?"

"Yes, he bought a new suitcase in San Antonio and so asked me for another tag."

Dr. Lipscomb sat on the edge of his chair and resumed the gentle tapping of his finger tips. "Might that tag not have been planted there by the murderer in order to throw suspicion on one of my guests?" he asked. "Anyone about the hotel could have picked one up."

"That is possible, Dr. Lipscomb, but scarcely probable, I think."

The beat of Lipscomb's fingertips was gradually increasing in tempo. "I read a brief account of the murder in one of the newspapers down here," he said. "I understood that a window of the murdered man's room opened out onto a fire escape and that this window was open. Is that true?"

"Yes."

"Then I can see no reason, beyond this matter of the luggage tag, for believing that anyone registered in the hotel committed the murder."

"It happened," Rennert said, "that this fire escape had been painted the day before and that the paint had not yet entirely dried.

There were no footprints on the paint. No one went through that window."

"Oh!" Dr. Lipscomb's fingers were still for an instant

"I should like to know," Rennert asked, "why you did not investigate Payne's whereabouts when he failed to join you the morning you left."

"Because of his note."

"His note?" Rennert's eyes narrowed slightly.

"Yes." Lipscomb's fingers were fluttering now.

"When I arose I found a note from him which had been slipped under my door. In it he said that he had found that it was impossible for him to accompany us to Mexico and that he had left the hotel."

"You did not suspect a forgery?"

"Of course not. I had never seen the man's handwriting."

Rennert crushed his cigarette into the ashtray. "Do you have a list of the members of your party?" he asked.

"Yes, of course."

"Might I see it?"

"Certainly." Dr. Lipscomb arose and went to the dresser on the other side of the room. "I should tell you," he said as he drew a brief case from one of the drawers, "that we do not call those who join our tours 'members of the party' but 'guests.' It helps create the atmosphere of comradeship and good feeling for which the Inter-America Tours stand."

"Thank you, Doctor. I shall remember in the future."

Dr. Lipscomb extended a long, official-looking sheet of white paper.

"This is the blanket passport which the Mexican government gives me for my guests. It saves them the trouble of securing individual tourist certificates. You will find each person's name listed here, his age, his address and his occupation."

Rennert took the paper, glanced down it. "Thirteen," he commented.

"No, no, fourteen, Mr. Rennert. I include myself, you see." Dr. Lipscomb sat down, smiled weakly. "I have found that travelers frequently have a superstitious aversion to the number thirteen, so I say that there are fourteen of us. You understand?"

"Yes, I understand," Rennert murmured.

For the moment he was oblivious of Dr. Lipscomb as his eyes ran down the list of names upon the paper.

Here was the name of a person who had escaped detection in the United States and Mexico, for whom young Payne had spent months in searching. A person who had choked Payne to death as calmly as he would have wrung the neck of a chicken. A person who was engaged, as a certain high official in the Mexican government had so eloquently expressed it, in "looting the centuries." Rennert's finger wavered a trifle as it passed from name to name. He still saw Payne's young face as it had looked up at him from that slab in the San Antonio morgue.

NAME	AGE	ADDRESS	OCCUPATION
Stephen Endicott Willis	65	St. Louis, Mo.	jeweler
Henrietta Stark Willis	63	St. Louis, Mo.	wife
Sarah Ernestine Tredkin	54	Wichita, Kansas	none
Francis Requa Tancel	29	Kansas City, Mo.	artist
James Hopkins Brody	58	Amarillo, Texas	rancher
Horace Starns Bymaster	46	Denver, Colorado	professor
Edward Lee Earp	32	Chicago, Ill.	broker
Mary Jane Earp	26	Chicago, Ill.	wife
Gertrude Estelle Dean	25	Fort Worth, Texas	teacher
Josephine Bernadine McCool	25	Fort Worth, Texas	teacher
Richard Armstead Enloe	67	Oklahoma City, Okla.	Colonel (retired) U.S. Army
Priscilla Evans Rankin	52	St. Louis, Mo.	none
Ricardo Montellano Argudin	35	New York, N. Y.	promoter

Rennert's eyes rose from the paper.

"Were you acquainted with any of these people before the tour started, Dr. Lipscomb?"

"With only one. Mrs. Rankin, of St. Louis. This is her third trip to Mexico as a guest of the Inter-America Tours." His thin, precise voice stressed the "third."

Rennert repeated it to himself. A little stab of excitement went through him. A third trip. "Makes regular trips back and forth across the border as a member of tourist parties," Payne had written. Rennert's eyes were again on the twelfth line of the paper.

Priscilla Evans Rankin.

"And Mrs. Rankin's husband?" he inquired.

"She is a widow. Her husband, I believe, died in Mexico a number of years ago. She lives quietly by herself in St. Louis. Once a year, at the same time, she comes to Mexico. She says she finds it more restful than a long ocean trip and a more interesting country than any which she has visited." Dr. Lipscomb's head nodded, as if in approbation of Mrs. Rankin's judgment.

And, Rennert told himself, that was that. He could scarcely picture Mrs. Rankin . . .

"All these people were registered at the Patio Hotel on the night of October 7th?" he asked.

"All except Mr. Brody. He joined us at the station."

"Your tour starts from St. Louis, I understand. The others joined you either there or en route?"

"Mr. Argudin was registered at the hotel when we arrived. The others joined us at various places."

"How long were you in San Antonio?"

"A day and a night. We spent the day sightseeing."

"Did Payne meet your other guests, Dr. Lipscomb?"

"Yes," Dr. Lipscomb fixed his gaze upon the chandelier, "I believe he met all of them. Except Mr. Brady, of course. He accompanied us on our sightseeing during the afternoon."

"Did he seem to be interested in anyone of them in particular?" Rennert studied the other's face as he asked the question.

Dr. Lipscomb made a vague gesture with his right hand.

"Not that I remember, but he may have done so. There was so much confusion—"

"Yes, of course." Rennert ran a finger over the fop of the sheet of paper. "Do you have another copy of this?"

"Yes."

"Might I have it?"

"Certainly."

Dr. Lipscomb walked to the dresser, took another typewritten sheet of paper from the brief case and handed it to Rennert.

Rennert stood up and returned the original passport.

"Do you have any objections," he asked, "if I join your party— become one of your guests rather," he amended hastily, "for the rest of this trip?"

For a moment Dr. Lipscomb seemed nonplused.

"Why no," he managed at last. "I shall be glad to have you. Do I understand that you want to make an investigation among my guests?"

"Yes."

He thrust a hand into a pocket and took a few paces toward the window. "I cannot permit my guests to be molested by questioning, you understand," he said, turning to Rennert.

Rennert smiled. "My identity will remain a secret between you and me. I shall try to make my questions discreet and shall not annoy any of the other guests."

Dr. Lipscomb shrugged a shoulder.

"Very well, then, Mr. Rennert. You are staying in this hotel?"

"Yes. Are all of your guests here?"

"Yes."

"Then I'll say good night, Dr. Lipscomb." His hand on the knob of the door, Rennert turned, a smile playing about the corners of his lips.

"What's on the program for tomorrow?"

"We go to Xochimilco. The cars will leave from the hotel at eight o'clock sharp."

"Good. I'll be there."

He opened the door and came face to face with the glowing end of a cigarette, that illuminated the dark oval face of a man somewhat shorter than Rennert. This man took the cigarette from his lips, smiled slightly and bowed.

"Pardon," he said softly.

Dr. Lipscomb stepped forward.

"Oh, come in, Mr. Argudin. This is Mr. Rennert, who has decided to become one of my guests."

"A pleasure, Mr. Rennert." Argudin's hand met Rennert's. It was small and cold and singularly lifeless. His petal-shaped black eyes met Rennert's for an instant, then looked past him at Dr. Lipscomb. "He takes the place of the young man whom we left in San Antonio?"

A frown flitted across Dr. Lipscomb's smooth forehead.

"In a way, yes.

"Then we shall hope," Argudin said, smoothing with one finger the end of his silky black mustache, "that he does not decide to leave us—so suddenly."

"Thank you," Rennert said. "I do not intend to."

With another bow, Argudin stepped across the threshold and closed the door.

In the dimly lighted hallway, Rennert stopped to examine for a moment the sheet of paper which Dr. Lipscomb had given him. When he folded it and placed it carefully in his pocket, opposite three names thereon were small check marks. The names were those of the men to whom Dr. Lipscomb had handed out luggage tags in San Antonio, therefore the men most likely to have been carrying one of them in a pocket—Mr. Brody, Mr. Earp—and Mr. Argudin.

5
IN THIS ROOM

THAT MORNING Rennert did a rare thing. He permitted himself a certain amount of self-indulgence. In other words, he stood on the balcony outside his bedroom window and watched the sun rise over the volcanoes.

For, banked by the years beneath the ashes of self-restraint, Rennert's nature was a sentimental, not to say romantic, one. In his boyhood he had moved on the unstable heights of Scott and Byron; during his university days he had wavered between the magnet of poetry and sophomoric mysticism and that of stern reality which he saw awaiting him inexorably at the end of the college cloisters. It was at this formative period that he had first seen the sun rise over Popocatepetl and Ixtaccihuatl. Never, even in these later years when the vagaries of life had thrown him into a world where a man who mooned over mountains was, to say the least, "half cracked," had the image of those snows at dawn been entirely erased from his retina.

Now he stood in his dressing gown on the stone balcony and watched them again, saw the first ray strike the summit of Popo like a suddenly lighted beacon fire, gazed in rapture as the Sleeping Woman bared her white breasts. For a moment of breathless duration the two mates stood revealed in crystal clarity over the valley, then the mists began to creep upward like oceans of frothy milk. Popo and Ixtaccihuatl hung in the air, detached mountains of the moon. Then the moment was past and clouds covered the southeastern horizon.

A sneeze punctuated his descent to earth. He left the balcony, closed the window and mentally kicked himself. A middle-aged man with gray hair beginning to show at the temples standing for half an hour in a dressing gown and slippers watching a sunrise. He had probably taken cold and a cold at the elevation of Mexico City was no joking matter.

Yet self-reproach could not entirely dampen the thrill of exhilaration which ran through him as he dressed and descended to breakfast in the coffee room adjoining the hotel. Several of the breakfasters bore the unmistakable earmarks of tourists and he wondered, as he sipped the strong black coffee, whether they were of Dr. Lipscomb's flock.

At the news stand he bought a San Antonio paper of the day before and returned to his room to glance over it.

He was thus engaged when the maid, a short, heavy-set old woman, entered and crossed the room, a load of towels upon her arm. As she emerged from the bathroom Rennert turned to crush a cigarette in the ashtray beside his chair. He was in time to see her cross herself with a quick furtive movement.

His curiosity was piqued. "Why do you cross yourself?" he asked in Spanish.

She stood for a moment, her fingers twisting the fringe of a soiled towel, her face impassive. Her jet black eyes did not meet his.

"Why do you cross yourself?" he repeated, laying down his paper. "You fear?"

"No, *señor*," the clutch upon the towel tightened, "I do not fear, but one does not forget the dead. One prays that they may rest in peace."

"The dead? Has one died, then?"

"Yes, *señor*. In this room."

"When?" Despite himself, Rennert felt his pulse quicken. It was one of the disappointments of his life that, contrary to popular belief, melodrama had little place in his calling.

"It makes now many, many days ago. I do not remember how many. A man hung himself in this room," she gestured upward at the chandelier. "In this room he hung himself and they say he has found no rest. It is the *fiesta de los muertos* and I pray for his soul. *Con permiso, señor.*"

The voluminous folds of her dark skirts rustled like wind-blown leaves about her feet as she left the room.

La fiesta de los muertos! The holiday of the dead! Out of sheer satisfaction at the grim appropriateness of it all Rennert found himself whistling under his breath as he put on his overcoat. Some Aztec deity with a sense of humor must be looking over him, he told himself. The Eve of All Saints' Day—Halloween back home. In Mexico, the eve of the two-day festival of the ancient Goddess of Death—the Day of the Dead.

He cast a speculative look at the ornate crystal chandelier before he closed the door.

6
THE WATERS OF XOCHIMILCO

It was a few minutes before eight o'clock when Rennert emerged from the elevator into the lobby.

Dr. Lipscomb detached himself from a little group near the desk and approached, his smile wide, bland and beaming as he extended his hand.

"Good morning, Mr. Rennert. I wondered if you had forgotten our trip this morning. Sleep well? Come on and meet my other guests," a quick, perfunctory clasp of the hands and Dr. Lipscomb had him by the arm, propelling him across the floor. "We are just about ready to start. It looks as if we were going to have a fine day. I am sure that you will enjoy— Folks, I want you to meet a new guest who has just joined us. Mr. Rennert."

Rennert had a confused impression of being the center of interest, of shaking hands with an ill-defined circle of people.

Miss Tredkin, gray hair and a limp, dry hand; Colonel Enloe, erect shoulders and a sandy-colored, toothbrush mustache; Mr. Tancel, a high-pitched voice ("Delighted, Mr. Rennert") and a light pressure of fingertips; Mrs. Rankin, a little gray field mouse; Mr. Brody, a huge sombrero and a booming voice ("Mighty glad to know you, Mr. Rennert. Glad to have you with us,") and a grip which momentarily paralyzed his fingers; Professor Bymaster, a high white collar and a small hand which Rennert did not feel.

The introduction concluded, Dr. Lipscomb glanced nervously about the lobby.

"Anyone seen Miss Dean and Miss McCool?"

"I suppose they'll be late again," the thin voice was Miss Tredkin's. "What time is it, Doctor?"

"Eight o'clock sharp. The cars are waiting for us outside."

"Aren't the Willises and the Earps going, Doc?" Brody asked.

"No, Mr. Willis isn't feeling well this morning. The Earps said that they preferred to—to sleep."

There was a snicker from someone, Mr. Tancel it seemed. Brody winked at Dr. Lipscomb.

"Honeymooners don't give you much trouble, do they, Doc?"

Two tiny spots of red appeared on Dr. Lipscomb's cheeks. He turned away.

"Here they come now," he said with evident relief, at the sight of two girls who were breathlessly steering a passage across the lobby. "Let's be going."

"Sorry to keep you waiting," the girls chimed as they approached.

The party, under the tow of Dr. Lipscomb, had started for the doorway and the rite of introduction with the newcomers was neglected. Of Miss Dean and Miss McCool Rennert only grasped the fact that one was rather tall and thin, the other short and plump.

Outside the hotel there ensued a brief period of confusion, while the seemingly momentous problem of the seating arrangement in the three shining Buicks was being decided. Rennert found himself in the last car, occupying the front seat which Miss Tredkin had chosen after much deliberation and then vacated for a rear seat in another car. Behind him sat Tancel, between Miss Dean and Miss McCool, the alacrity with which they had descended upon these places denoting, Rennert told himself, a preconcerted understanding.

The driver, a young Mexican, turned an imperturbable face in the direction of Dr. Lipscomb, nodded, and they were off.

"For God's sake give me a cigarette!" one of the girls exclaimed.

"At your service, my fair lady," from Tancel.

Rennert from the corner of his eye watched the three light cigarettes.

"I was scared to death that old hen Tredkin was going to ride in this car," the tall girl said, emitting a defiant cloud of smoke from her nostrils. "Remember how she glared at me when she saw me smoking on the train?"

"And, say, do you remember that time she came back in the diner and found us drinking wine?" Tancel's high-pitched voice tinkled into a laugh. "'Oh, Dr. Lipscomb,' she said, 'what are our young people coming to?'" There was a chorus of merriment at his mimicry.

One of the girls leaned over in front of Tancel and said something to the other. Rennert was aware of a feeling of restraint and of a low-pitched conversation.

He felt a yank at his sleeve, which had been resting upon the back of the seat, and turned to look into a pair of rather close-set gray-green eyes.

"Say," the tall girl said, "we haven't met you yet and this dumb-bell here," indicating Tancel, "has forgotten your name. I'm Jo McCool and my running mate over there is Gertrude Dean. We're schoolteachers from Texas, trying to forget our worries. You can have our life history later, if you want it."

Her wavy, light brown hair flowed from under a green tam-o'-shanter perched at a rakish angle upon her head. When she smiled, as she was doing now, the sharp lines of her face seemed to pucker and her eyes to narrow. Her head moved from side to side with startling abruptness as she talked—like, Rennert told himself, a startled canary.

He smiled his most engaging smile.

"Rennert's the name. From New York. Just another tourist. Glad to know you folks."

"We're just one great big happy family, you know, Mr. Rennert. At least that's what Daddy Lipscomb says," the other girl said. She was dressed in a tight fitting brown dress and her curves were accentuated, rather than hidden, by a scarf or shawl or sash (Rennert wasn't sure just what it was) around her waist. Her hair was closely bobbed and startlingly coppery.

"Have a cigarette?" Tancel extended a package. "Better smoke 'em while they last. American tobacco costs like the dickens down here and these two gold diggers are on my last carton."

Rennert accepted one and, as he cupped his hands against the wind, studied the donor.

Tancel was a tall young man, with a pale, bony, almost girlish face. His head was bare and the wind played with his long, curly blond locks. He wore brown and white plus-fours.

"You're late joining our party," he remarked. "You've missed seeing one hundred and fifty cathedrals, a dozen or two pyramids, the twenty-nine places where Cortes buried his wives—"

"Oh, yes," Miss McCool gave Rennert's sleeve another yank, "you just got here last night, didn't you? I saw you down in the lobby of the hotel. We were just passing out."

"Out is right," Tancel said and ducked to escape Miss McCool's elbow. "What a party! What a party!"

"Never again," Miss Dean raised a right hand toward heaven, "will I mix drinks. That absinthe!" She covered her face with her hands and rocked back and forth. "Oh, that absinthe!"

"And yet they say that absinthe makes the heart grow fonder."

Both girls joined in Tancel's laughter.

For a time thereafter Rennert passed out of their orbit. Their conversation became to him an unintelligible potpourri of wise-cracks and references to parties, past, present and future.

He gave his attention to the scenery and his thoughts to the other members of the party whom he had met in the lobby of the hotel. The henna-haired Miss Dean and the (what was the word?) pugnacious Miss McCool were, he had decided, off his list of sus-pects. About Tancel he reserved his judgment. He seemed an in-nocent enough young fellow, but Rennert had a deeply ingrained distrust of young fellows who were too obviously innocent. That fair-haired youth at the Canadian border that time, for instance. The scented soap in his bags had contained diamonds to the tune of $10,000. . . .

They were passing the Churubusco Country Club when Rennert was suddenly whirled again into their orbit.

The talk had veered to a discussion of the dark-haired Mr. Argudin, of whom Miss McCool was expressing her opinion in no uncertain terms.

"I don't know what Daddy Lipscomb ever let him in on this so-called 'select' party for. He makes me nervous when he looks at me with those little beady black eyes—"

Tancel doubled over with laughter. "Do you remember the day on the train when we were all getting acquainted and Miss Tredkin was being sociable and incidentally finding out all about everybody's business? And she said to him: 'What is your profession, Mr. Argudin?' Just like that—'What is your profession, Mr. Argudin?' And he smiled and said—"

Miss Dean sat up straight and contorted her round face into a semblance of Argudin's smile. "And he said: 'I am a dilettant, Miss Tredkin.'"

"And then she just sat and looked at him for a minute with her mouth open and got up and left," Tancel went off into incoherency.

"She told me later," Miss Dean's voice was a little shriek of hilarity, "that she didn't think he was a nice man."

"He's always pestering me to play bridge with him," Miss McCool managed to get in. "He wanted me to play with him last night, but I told him nothing doing;" her head was switching back and forth with pendulum-like regularity. "Not after that last night in San Antonio."

(Rennert always had an uneasy feeling that his ears actually stood out to a perceptible degree when something suddenly caught his attention.)

"You remember," Miss McCool's head bobbed toward Miss Dean, "that we played downstairs in that room off the lobby for four solid hours—from nine o'clock until one. We were playing for—what was it we were playing for? Oh, yes, a cent a point. I kept yawning and yawning, but he wouldn't take the hint. I never got so tired of bridge in my life, even though I won. And he's been after me ever since to play again. He's as persistent as that fellow in Dallas last Christmas. You remember, Gertie—"

And again Rennert was sitting in the front seat with a silent driver while behind him the three were in another sphere which revolved around some nightclub and a dispute about dances and what somebody said to somebody else.

The black-eyed Mr. Argudin was, then, accounted for on the night when Payne was murdered. Unless, of course, this bridge game had been some sort of prepared alibi. . . .

Rennert was still thinking about Mr. Argudin when the car rounded a curve, sped between adobe walls and past an aged cathedral, and drew up beside the other cars.

Dr. Lipscomb beckoned them toward the landing place, where a flower-decked *chalupa* awaited them.

Miss McCool and Miss Dean, each grasping one of Tancel's arms, took their places in the little wicker chairs which lined the boat.

The rest of the party sat in various attitudes of expectancy. Rennert and Dr. Lipscomb got in last, taking chairs near the prow. The bored-looking Indian at the other end thrust his pole into the water, heaved and the *chalupa* turned slowly around, heading down the canal.

Beauty beset them on every side in a riot of color. Scarlet poppies, shasta daisies white against green leaves, purple bougainvillea against a thatched roof, pink and yellow water lilies, pansies and carnations, slim tall poplars rising straight out of diminutive cornfields.

Rennert relaxed in his chair, vaguely conscious of Dr. Lipscomb's voice and of the rippling of the water as the boatman's pole splashed in and out. Someone had asked a question.

"No, these are not artificial canals but the remnants of the old lake which once covered this part of the Valley of Mexico. In the time of the Aztecs Mexico City, or Tenochtitlan as it was then called, was supplied with fruits and flowers and vegetables from Xochimilco. They were grown on floating rafts covered with earth. . . ."

On Rennert's left sat Miss McCool, Tancel and Miss Dean. Then Miss Tredkin.

Rennert studied the tall, thin Miss Tredkin. She sat stiffly erect upon the straight little chair, casting nervous glances at the water which lapped the sides of the boat. Her hands were clasped upon her lap. Against the pagan orgy of color her steel-gray hair confined by a severely plain straw hat, the black taffeta which sheathed her body, her lined face looked curiously out of place.

"These rafts were called *chinampas*," Dr. Lipscomb was continuing. "When the rest of the lake was drained, after the Conquest by the Spaniards, these floating rafts remained stationary and in the course of time were moored to the bottom by the roots of the plants."

A canoe, manned by a lithe Indian girl, darted out of a hidden waterway and approached them.

"*Claveles, señores*," the girl called, holding out a huge bouquet of pink carnations.

Mr. Brody, sitting next to Miss Tredkin, held out his hand. The girl passed them to him.

"*Cuánto?*" he asked.

"*Cincuenta centavos, señor.*"

"*Es mucho. Toma.*" He thrust a coin into her hands and turned his back.

"How much did you give her?" Miss Tredkin asked, eying the bouquet uncertainly.

"Forty *centavos*," Brody answered. "She wanted fifty."

"How much is that in our money?"

"Oh, about a dime. Want these?" He thrust them at her.

Miss Tredkin opened her mouth, closed it again, took the flowers and held them stiffly erect in her lap.

James Brody, rancher. Rennert gave Mr. Brody his attention. The tiny chair upon which he sat gave his frame gargantuan proportions. The buttons of his blue serge suit seemed on the point of bursting. His round red face wore an expression of pleasure, infantile almost, as he looked about him. From time to time, seemingly in sheer excess of animal spirits, he dipped a beefy hand over the side and watched the water run through his fingers. Rennert conjured up pictures of mustangs and mesquite bushes and alkali deserts and long-horned cattle.

Opposite Brody, at the far end of the boat, sat Mrs. Rankin. Remembering Dr. Lipscomb's words, Rennert looked at her again. A fragile little woman with pearl gray hair and a quietly beautiful face. She sat gazing backward at the ripples in their wake. One hand lay in her lap, a white petal against black silk.

Black silk. . . .

Rennert's eyes fell involuntarily.

Mrs. Rankin's dress was long and her shoes were high, but between them he saw the sheen of dark gray silk. Anything else, he told himself, would have jarred the discreet perfection of her dress.

Before Rennert had turned his attention to Professor Bymaster he knew that Miss Tredkin's thin limbs (to think even of "legs" in her connection would be a profanation) were covered with black wool and that Miss McCool's and Miss Dean's sheer, transparent hose probably bore some such name as "Moonlight" or "Fairy Webs."

"No, Miss Tredkin," Dr. Lipscomb's voice was patient, "there is no danger at all. These boats are well built, these men spend all their lives on these canals and are perfectly trustworthy. Besides, the water isn't deep. Yes, Miss Dean, those flowers are certainly beautiful.

"At Xochimilco, more than anywhere else, one can obtain an idea of the Mexican love for flowers and color. We of the United States cannot grasp it in its full significance—"

Next to Mrs. Rankin sat Professor Bymaster, his eyes, as he followed Dr. Lipscomb's discourse, seeming to stand out like two round brown berries behind his tortoise-shell spectacles. His high white collar held his small head poised at an uncomfortable looking angle, giving one the constant impression that he was about to say something, if the others would give him the opportunity.

Colonel Enloe sat next, both his physique (he was a tall, broad-shouldered man, pink-faced, with bushy eyelashes and small china blue eyes) and his manner and bearing, as he pulled importantly at the stiff bristles of his mustache, thrusting the diminutive professor into complete effacement.

And now, Rennert told himself as the boat glided back toward the landing, he had met all his suspects, with the exception of the two married couples at the hotel. He felt oddly exhilarated, whether with the mountain air, heady as clear cool wine, or with the excitement of the chase before him, he could not have told.

They returned by way of Coyoacan and San Angel.

The conversation on the rear seat consisted principally of ecstatic discussion of the morning's boat ride and of the other members of the party, interrupted at frequent intervals by ejaculations as they passed a bougainvillea-covered wall, a flower-filled patio, or a crumbling church.

Rennert was engaged in assorting his impressions of the morning and in agreeing to Miss McCool's and Miss Dean's comments on the landscape when an incident occurred which suddenly concentrated his attention on Tancel.

They were passing through the narrow streets of San Angel when Miss Dean asked:

"Isn't this the place where we came and looked at all those horrid old skeletons and things under the lava?"

"Yes," Tancel replied, gesturing toward the massive Carmelite church, "the entrance is back there, you remember." his lips, usually occupied with a cigarette, in its absence were half open with a curious expression of eagerness.

"What did Daddy Lipscomb tell us that we ought to remember about those old bones?"

"They are the oldest remains of human occupation in the Valley of Mexico. Mount Ajusco over there erupted and spread lava over this part of the country to the depth of from five to twenty feet. Under this lava, out there in the Pedregal, a cemetery has been discovered, at least two thousand years old—"

Tancel stopped suddenly and fumbled in his pocket for a package of cigarettes.

"Why, Francis," Miss McCool jerked her head in his direction and opened her eyes in affected astonishment, "you talk like Daddy Lipscomb. I didn't know you knew all that stuff."

"Well, you see," the young man said hastily, "I've read quite a bit about Mexico and have been here before. I didn't mean to go spouting off like that, though—"

Rennert had turned in his seat.

"I didn't know that you had been here before," he said casually. "When were you here last?"

"Last summer. I was in the summer school of the National University." Tancel turned abruptly to Miss McCool. "Are we going to the Frontón tonight?"

"What do you say, Gertie? Want to go?"

And Rennert gazed at lofty Chapultepec through narrowed eyes. Had Tancel betrayed himself by showing too much knowledge? Or was his obvious embarrassment at his slip due to the pose which he, like so many young men, affected of indifference to anything but the froth of life?

They whirled down the Paseo de la Reforma and drew up at the hotel.

Dr. Lipscomb called them and they joined the little group about him.

"Wednesday night," the conductor said, "I am having a little farewell dinner party and should like all of you to be my guests. It will, you know, be our last night in Mexico City. Also, the management of the hotel has asked me to announce that there will be a masquerade ball that night, to which you are all invited."

They scattered then and Rennert made his way into the lobby and to the desk, where he found Dr. Lipscomb conversing with two women and two men. The conductor hailed him.

"Mr. Rennert, I want you to meet these people. Mr. and Mrs. Willis—" Rennert shook hands with a solid-appearing man of medium height, whose sparse gray hair was plastered down upon his head, and with an even more solid-appearing woman, dressed in a smart blue suit and wide-brimmed hat, "and Mr. and Mrs. Earp." Earp was tall, with a well proportioned, athletic figure, and his hand met Rennert's with a firm grip. His long, slightly chevaline, face was pink and glowing, as if he had just shaven. His wife was a plump little blonde, with round blue eyes and fluffy flaxen hair. Her voice, as she replied to Rennert's greeting, had a faint suggestion of a lisp.

"We were just going down to Sanborn's for tea," Willis said to Dr. Lipscomb. "Will you join us?"

"Sorry, Mr. Willis, but I cannot right now. I have some business to attend to."

"Do you want to go with us, Mr. Rennert?"

"I don't believe so, Mr. Willis. Thank you."

"Mr. Rennert?" He turned to the clerk who had addressed him. "Yes."

"A telegram for you."

Rennert took the envelope and tore it open.

The Willises and the Earps had started toward the door.

Rennert's lips were pursed as he read the message. He put it in his pocket and hurriedly followed the departing tourists. On the sidewalk outside he stepped up to them.

"Do you mind," he asked, "if I change my mind and go with you?"

7
TEA AT SANBORN'S

"*TE Y PASTEL, señorita, por favor.*"

The dark-eyed little Aztec waitress flashed a teeth-revealing smile at Rennert (largesse for his use of the soft Mexican tongue in this place of terrifying consonants) and vanished.

"A beautiful place," Willis commented as his tired brown eyes took in the ancient carved pillars of the patio, dull against blue and white majolica, the feathery geyser of the fountain. The soft, glass-filtered light seemed to smooth out his deeply lined face and to relax the firm set of his thin lips. "So restful. I hadn't imagined there was a place like this in Mexico." He removed his white gold eye-glasses and passed a hand over lowered lids.

"This is your first visit to Mexico, Mr. Willis?" Rennert asked.

"Yes."

"Mr. Willis' first vacation in years," his wife said, turning her soft, dark gray eyes on Rennert. (Pleasant, motherly eyes, he told himself, oddly at variance with the chiseled hardness of her full face.) "He has been awfully busy lately and worried, you know, about business, so I told him that he ought to take a week or so off and come to Mexico or some place and just—ah—" her mouth remained open.

There was a moment of silence.

"Relax," suggested Rennert.

"Yes, relax, and forget his troubles."

Earp, seated across the table in the close, intimate little booth, rested an elbow on the mosaic of the top and gazed absently into the wavering cloud of smoke which ascended from his cigarette. His slate-blue eyes had a dreamy expression.

Mrs. Earp sat close to him, one round shoulder (cream beneath the skim milk of a diaphanous blue dress) pressed against the gray tweed of his arm. The clarity of her complexion and the redness of her full lips were due, Rennert decided, to art rather than to nature. Her face had the innocent placidity of a doll's and all of a doll's brittle hardness. Rennert found himself gazing abstractedly at the small diamond in the tarnished band of gold which encircled the third finger of her left hand.

"You've been in Mexico before, Rennert?" Earp asked.

Rennert looked up. "Yes." (Maybe it was the glittering coldness concentrated in the stone, accentuated by contrast with the dull dead metal. He had never liked diamonds.) "I have been here before."

Aware that nothing inspires confidence like confidence, he proceeded to give a fully detailed, entirely plausible account of an imaginary business trip.

"We talked about going to Canada for our honeymoon," Earp said, "but decided we'd be different and come to Mexico. I'm a broker, in a small way, in Chicago and wanted a change. We're not sorry we came here, are we, honey?" He cast a sideways glance at the blue eyes by his side.

"Of course not," the blue eyes returned the glance. "It's an absolutely perfect place." The lisp was more noticeable now.

"Mr. Willis is in the jewelry business—in St. Louis," Mrs. Willis said. "Of course it's not necessary for him to be in the store all the time, but he just won't leave it. I tell him that he is getting to an age when he ought to rest and play more, drop the—"

"The reins," her husband automatically supplied. "Yes, the reins, a little."

The waitress set tea and sandwiches and pastry before them.

"Oh, look, Ed," Mrs. Earp nudged her husband, "at that perfectly gorgeous fur that woman over there has on."

"Just keep your eyes on this gorgeous food here," he replied, a grin playing about the corners of his mouth. It relieved a certain metallic tightness about the lines of his long face and gave him a pleasant, almost boyish expression. He winked at Rennert. "Not married, are you, Rennert? You ought to be glad, because women are death on furs. Why, I got stuck for a fur coat on our way down here. The wife saw a sale of them in San Antonio and talked me into buying her one. And then," he chuckled, "we found that we didn't have room enough for it in our luggage, so had to buy a new suitcase. And now she's got her eyes on more furs!"

"Aw, Ed!" his wife gently shoved a plump elbow into his side.

"By the way," Mrs. Willis asked, "do you know how much stuff we are allowed to take across the border without paying duty, Mr. Rennert?"

Rennert dropped another piece of sugar into his tea, watched it dissolve.

"One hundred dollars' worth, I believe," he said.

"I wanted to get some linen down here and was afraid I'd have to pay duty on it."

Rennert looked up. "One hundred dollars will buy a great deal of linen, Mrs. Willis."

Her attention was concentrated on a chocolate éclair. "Oh, I won't have anything near that much, of course. I need some new linen, though, and it's so cheap down here and I want to take back some presents to some of my friends, something unusual, some-thing—"

"Distinctive?" Rennert suggested, after an instant.

"Yes, distinctive." She turned to her husband. "I wouldn't eat any more of that pastry, if I were you, Stephen. It's very rich. You know, Mr. Rennert, Mr. Willis has to be so careful about what he eats. That is one reason why we hesitated about coming to Mexico. We weren't sure about the food. He hasn't had any trouble, though, except when we were coming through San Antonio. He ate some Mexican food in a restaurant, said he just wanted to see what it tasted like. It didn't agree with him."

Mr. Willis had laid down his fork and was clipping the end from a cigar.

"Oh, did you folks stop in San Antonio?" Rennert asked casually.

"Yes, we spent a day there, seeing the sights." Willis drew from his pocket a box of diminutive wax matches, struck one futilely, tossed it into the tray.

"I remember now that Dr. Lipscomb did say you had stopped there." Rennert put down his cup. "There was some kind of excitement in your hotel, wasn't there? A murder, I believe?"

The clatter of Mrs. Willis' spoon against her plate punctuated the stillness.

"A murder?" Mrs. Earp's eyes were two round blue agates. Her shoulder pressed more closely against the gray tweed. "Oh, Ed, we didn't hear about that!"

"I read something about it in the paper down here," Willis looked at Rennert over the unsteady flame of his second match, "but didn't pay much attention. What were the particulars?"

"I don't know. I haven't seen a paper lately. Dr. Lipscomb just happened to mention it."

Willis applied the flame to the end of his cigar, puffed contentedly a moment and placed the match in the tray.

"Your city of Chicago doesn't seem to have a monopoly on gangsters, does it, Earp?" he smiled.

"This may have been a graduate of Chicago." Earp turned to Rennert. "Was it a shooting?"

"I believe," Rennert said, "that it was a case of strangulation—with a pair of silk stockings."

"Silk stockings!" Earp cleared his throat, grinned at Willis. "It wasn't a Chicago killing, then. Our gangsters use machine guns. Strangling is too slow."

"Howdy, folks!" Miss McCool and Miss Dean, with Tancel in tow, passed their table with a waving of hands.

"There go the school marms," Earp laughed, "with their sucker."

"Maybe," his wife suggested, a little dimple appearing in her round chin, "they're the suckers. You see," she explained to the others, "the McCool girl has just oodles of money."

"She has?" Mrs. Willis' eyebrows were raised a trifle.

"Yes, she was a school teacher in some small town in Texas. Then her uncle or her grandfather or something died and left her all his money—oil, I think it was. She quit teaching and is trying to spend some of her money seeing Life (she pronounces it just that way—with a capital L) before it's too late. She'd better hurry."

"Meouw," from her husband behind cupped hands. Oblivious, Mrs. Earp went on:

"The other girl, Miss Dean, is an old friend of hers, so she got her to come along on this trip. Miss McCool is paying all the expenses for her, I understand. They say—"

"Come on, let's be going," Earp interrupted. "The first thing you know these folks will think you're gossiping."

"Why, Ed, I'm not gossiping, but everybody knows that that Tancel fellow hasn't any money and that—"

Earp motioned to the waitress, who brought the checks.

Rennert placed a silver peso on the tray and became intent on contemplation of the flamboyant Orozco mural over the staircase. Not, however, before he had seen Willis take from his pocket a large billfold of brown alligator skin and extract therefrom a five peso bill.

I was right, he was saying to himself, *it was a man who bought those silk stockings and, unless something is very rotten indeed in the state of Texas, that man was our friend Mr. Willis.*

For the telegram in his pocket was from Inspector Miles in San Antonio and read:

CLERK IN DEPARTMENT STORE DESCRIBES
MAN TO WHOM SHE SOLD PAIR BLACK SILK
STOCKINGS LATE IN AFTERNOON OCTOBER
TWENTY-SIXTH MEDIUM HEIGHT GRAY HAIR
ABOUT SEVENTY YEARS OLD WHITE GOLD EYE-
GLASSES BROWN EYES WEARING DARK BLUE
SUIT CARRIED BILLFOLD ALLIGATOR SKIN.

8
OPEN TOMBS

HALF AN HOUR LATER Rennert sat in an uncomfortable Empire chair in the office of a certain high official of the Mexican government and smoked a fragrant black cigar.

The high official of the Mexican government—a short, heavily built man with a drooping mustache which made up in waxed blackness what it lacked in number of hairs—was stolid of face and manner, only his glowing black eyes and the quick, darting movements of his hands as he talked betraying his inner agitation.

"But, Mr. Rennert," he was saying in his precise English, which indicated its exoticism by its too great precision, by its soft lingering upon the vowels, by an occasional misplaced accent, "the affair becomes serious."

"Yes?" Rennert carefully deposited the ash from his cigar in the lap of a squatting idol of brown sandstone.

"More reports have come in. These—how you call them? Ghouls?"

Rennert nodded. "Ghouls will do."

"These ghouls have been at work during the summer, the rainy season, when their work is difficult but they are not disturbed." He leaned forward and continued in a softly audible voice: "A tomb in Oaxaca, one in Michoacán, another in the Distrito Federal—not ten miles from the capital! Open!"

"You have posted guards?"

"Of course. But it is useless. Our country it is so large. And there is bribery of the guards. And," the dark eyes were fixed on Rennert's

60

face, "among the ignorant ones, the country people, there are strange rumors. In Oaxaca the story goes about that the old kings are returning after their sleep of centuries—to sit upon their thrones. It is said that in Tzintzuntzan the Tarascans wait for their ancient capital to be established again. You understand," his eyelids fell slowly, "the danger—to us."

The smoke of Rennert's cigar was wafted lazily upward in the still air. His gaze followed the vagrant spirals

"I am satisfied," he said, "that the directing genius of this business is in Mexico City now, with this tourist party. By the time we cross the border again into Texas I hope to have proof enough to arrest him."

"You know who he is?"

"I have—suspicions."

"Then why not arrest him now?"

"This person is a citizen of the United States and committed a murder in the United States. Arrest in the United States for that crime will serve both purposes—yours and ours."

"There are ways," the other suggested, his fingers toying with an onyx inkstand, "to make a man talk."

"Yes, but there would be international complications and neither you nor I have evidence to connect anyone in this party with this business down here."

A brown palm gestured upward. "Very well, Mr. Rennert. We are leaving it in your hands. We shall aid you in any way possible."

"I should like some men, some secret service men—you have them, I suppose?—to shadow some of these people."

"Very well, Mr. Rennert. It shall be arranged."

Rennert arose (Damn Maximilian, he thought, for these chairs!) and took the other's extended hand.

"*Adios, señor.*"

"*Adios, señor* Rennert."

9
MEMENTO MORI

AFTER DINNER Rennert strolled hack toward the hotel, his thoughts on Mr. Willis.

A jeweler (the thought stuck). Yes, that fitted.

In appearance, a spruce American business man. Traveling for the rest, hence an explanation for failure to accompany the others on their sight-seeing trips.

A man, probably, who would see the opportunities in systematizing and carrying through on a large scale what for years had been a small but lucrative business, with few risks.

The special knowledge? Probably not so much of that was necessary. His agents in Mexico would have that. He would handle the United States end.

But those stockings! Identification had been too easy. . . .

Rennert crossed the Cinco de Mayo and entered the Telegraph Building, where he spent some time in the composition of a message.

When he came out he felt safer. It would not do to be too confident in Willis' guilt. Better not risk a false step. He knew that his telegram would set in motion an exhaustive investigation of the past activities of Mr. Stephen E. Willis, of St. Louis.

He strolled through the Alameda, the severely classic contours of its shrubbery and statuary now grotesquely distorted by flickering gasoline torches where men were at work erecting stalls for the fiesta of the next two days. Brown little gnomes out of some old German fairy tale, busy with hammer and nails. A marble nymph, metamorphosed by a bootblack's crayon into a Hollywood movie queen, clasped Grecian drapery about her breasts and gazed with terror at the profanation of her retreat.

Several *puestos* were already doing business, the vendors' cries—"*comidas para los muertos*," "*juguetes para los muertos*" ("food and toys for the dead")—ringing frantically through the hubbub.

In front of a toy booth Rennert caught sight of a familiar figure and approached.

Jim Brody, his sombrero pushed back on his head, was engaged in a vociferous, good-natured argument with a smiling woman whose wares—dancing skeletons whose wooden bones rattled realistically; purple candy funerals; stickpins in the shape of skull and crossbones, with gleaming ruby eyes—were spread out before her.

"*Cómprelos, cómprelos, señor*," she urged, "*son muy bonitos.*"

Brody caught sight of Rennert and turned, throwing an arm over his shoulder.

"Why, howdy, Rennert, old man! How's things?" Rennert smiled and returned the greeting, sniffed the odor of beer.

"Just buying some toys for my kids—something to take home, you know." Brody released his grip of Rennert's shoulder and picked up a handful of toys. "Junior'll have a fit when he sees this one." He released the spring of a jumping jack and burst into laughter when the legs and arms began to execute a lively dance.

He tossed a bill upon the board which served as Counter.

"*Tomo éstos*," he said to the woman.

Rennert had started to turn away when he stopped, suddenly fascinated by a little wooden figure which hung from the roof of the stall. It was a tiny skeleton of white, bare bones which danced and waved a bottle of tequila before his eyes. What attracted Rennert was the face. Thereon some native artist had epitomized the spirit of roguery—the sly, mocking smile of the bared teeth; the hideous emptiness of the nose, the eye sockets, out of which peeped a pair of the happiest, most mischievous eyes imaginable.

He took it down, gazed at it a moment, then gave the woman a coin.

She took it, gestured toward the toy. "*Guárdelo bien, señor. Se llama ci cuarto mago.*"

Rennert chuckled, then, out of pure joy.

"What did she say?" Brody asked. "My Spanish fails me."

"She told me," Rennert said, "to take good care of this little fellow. He is named 'the fourth wise man.'"

Brody laughed boisterously.

"Great people, these Mexicans! Make a joke out of everything."

Side by side they strolled across the Alameda.

"Wish I'd brought the kids down here," Brody said suddenly. "All these toys would have tickled 'em to death. I'd like to see Junior on one of those big straw horses." He grinned at the thought. "I'm going to get him a real pony his next birthday. I've got three of 'em, Rennert, the greatest little rascals you ever saw. Ever out in West Texas? You ought to come out sometime. Great country. Times have changed, though, since they've hit oil. It's not the same. What about a drink, old man?" They were passing the swinging doors of a cantina. "No? Well, drink one on me some other time. I'm going to take one more before I go to bed. You see," he pulled his sombrero forward over his forehead, "it's kind of lonesome running around here all by myself. I don't seem to hit it off with the rest of this bunch. Well, so long, Rennert. Be seein' you."

His broad back momentarily blotted out the garish light from within the *cantina*.

Rennert thoughtfully pursued his way to the hotel.

In a far corner of the lobby he caught sight of Miss Tredkin seated in solitary state, her thin erect shoulders against the tooled leather back of the chair. The rays of the reading lamp fell over her left shoulder on the book which she held in her hands. She did not look up as he passed her on his way to the stairs.

In the card room off the mezzanine floor Mr. and Mrs. Willis, Colonel Enloe and Argudin were playing bridge.

Rennert strolled past and glanced about for an unoccupied chair. Midway down the hall he paused.

In a little alcove partly masked by brocaded green curtains Mrs. Rankin sat upon a plush and gilt sofa.

In the softly shaded light from the solitary lamp her face had a peaceful, cameo-like perfection against pearl-gray hair. She sat stiffly erect, her hands folded upon her lap and her eyes fixed upon the sky visible through the French doors. Rennert stood in the doorway, oddly moved at the scene. A stage set, he thought, in which this *princesse lointaine* grown old was waiting for someone to make an entrance. . . .

He started to walk on, but at the sound of his feet on the soft rug she turned her face in his direction, smiled.

"Good evening, Mr. Rennert." Her voice had the soft yet impersonal sound of a bell in a mountain church, heard at a distance.

"Good evening, Mrs. Rankin." Despite himself, Rennert felt himself bowing slightly.

"Won't you come in and sit down?"

He hesitated. "Are you expecting someone?"

"Yes," her eyes met his, "but I have waited a long time. You do not disturb me, Mr. Rennert."

He crossed the room, sat on the sofa by her side. She did not change her position, but turned her head slightly in his direction.

"I was just looking," she said, "at the stars. They seem so near, here in Mexico."

"The old peoples, the Aztecs and the Mayas, must have had the same feeling. Their temples were oriented by the constellations. As truly as if by modern instruments."

"And now they orient their lives by them."

"Yes, the stars, the sun and the moon, the rains and the droughts—as universal a rhythm as Life and Death."

She looked at him for a long time without speaking. "You talk, Mr. Rennert," she said, "as if you had thought or lived a great deal. You are not an old man."

"One's life is not measured by years, Mrs. Rankin."

"True," her eyes wandered again to the window, "then I do not bore you?"

"No, Mrs. Rankin."

Silence fell between them. The sound of voices outside came softly, as if muffled by a great distance. The little platinum watch upon her wrist ticked dispassionately.

Rennert, fingering idly the painted toy, felt stealing over him a curious relaxation of the senses and, at the same time, was vaguely aware of tension—whether in himself or in the strangely quiet little lady by his side he could not have told.

His finger released the spring at the base of the toy. Instantly the little skeleton jumped into life, began his macabre dance. The left hand jerked the bottle to his lips, the right hand fell to his side. The right hand waggishly thumbed a nose, the left hand fell to his side. The roguish eyes looked into Rennert's.

A boon companion, he mused, with an invitation. *Memento mori.* There flashed across his memory a steel engraving (Was it by Doré?) in an old book which as a boy he had found in the attic. A grim, frightful old man with a long white beard. In one hand he held a scythe, its edge curved like his nose. With the other he beckoned inexorably. Rennert remembered waking in the middle of the night bathed in cold sweat while he stared into the darkness at the foot of the bed, where the old man had been standing. Yet the next day, with perverse eagerness, he had stolen up the attic stairs, gazed again at the picture.

"Here," Mrs. Rankin spoke quietly, as if she divined his thoughts, "and perhaps no place else on earth, there is no fear of death."

"Familiarity breeds contempt—even of death."

"And yet it is not dressed up with pretty stories about compensation. Here the grave is its goal."

"And here, if any place, I have often thought that the dead should be near to the living, like the stars."

She looked at him quickly, seemed to be studying his face.

"You have thought that, too?"

"Often. Ever since the first time I saw a Mexican family eating a picnic on the grave of a loved one, in happy communion with the dead."

Mrs. Rankin's white fingers were pressed tightly together, so that tiny blue veins stood out under the skin.

"Tomorrow and day after tomorrow," she said, "are the Days of the Dead. If ever they return it will be then."

Rennert met her eyes. "You are waiting for that, Mrs. Rankin?"

She smiled and a faint glow was on each cheek. "Yes, Mr. Rennert, I am waiting."

Still smiling, she turned her face to the window again.

"Mr. Rennert," a voice spoke from the doorway. He looked up, conscious of a feeling of annoyance, of anger almost, at the interruption.

Dr. Lipscomb stood there, a hand on either curtain. "Could I see you a few minutes, Mr. Rennert?"

"Certainly."

He arose, turned to his companion.

"You will pardon me, Mrs. Rankin?"

"Yes, Mr. Rennert. Good night."

"Good night, Mrs. Rankin."

He followed Dr. Lipscomb to chairs in a secluded spot.

"The first chance I have had to talk to you today, Mr. Rennert," Lipscomb said abruptly. "Have you—found out anything?"

Rennert shook his head.

"Not yet—nothing definite."

The conductor frowned, pulled his chair closer. "I've been thinking about what you told me last night and I feel surer than ever that you are making a mistake, a big mistake, Mr. Rennert. A murderer in my party! Why, it's preposterous! Do you still want to continue your investigation?"

"Yes, Dr. Lipscomb, I do."

"Well, as I told you, I want to help you in every way I can but I certainly wish that you would be reasonable about this. If my guests were to find out who you are, it would ruin me." He shifted his position nervously. "I am afraid they may find out."

Rennert glanced at him quickly. "Why?"

"You know how people are on these tours—everybody wants to know everybody else's business. Several of them have been asking me about you—who you are, where you are from, and so forth."

"Who has been asking?"

"Why, several of them. Just out of curiosity, I'm sure. Mr. Willis asked me about you tonight, said he liked you very much and wanted to know you better. And Colonel Enloe asked if you had been an army man."

"An army man?" Rennert frowned.

"Yes, he said there was something about your manner that made him think maybe you had been in the service—sort of an official manner, he called it."

"And you told him—?"

"That I didn't know much about you except that you were in business in New York."

"Did that seem to satisfy him?"

"I don't know. Someone came up just then and nothing more was said." Lipscomb glanced at his watch, got to his feet. "Well, I must make arrangements for tomorrow. We are going to the Pyramids. I suppose you will accompany us?"

"Are all the others going?"

"All except Mrs. Rankin, I believe. And Mr. Argudin."

Rennert considered.

"Yes," he said, "I shall go with you."

10
THE PYRAMIDS OF SAN JUAN TEOTIHUACAN

"OH!" MISS TREDKIN EMITTED what, had it proceeded from Miss McCool or Miss Dean, would have been inelegantly classified as a squeak, and gazed upward at the soaring flights of steps cut in the face of the terraced Pyramid of the Sun. "I could never climb that."

"Come on, come on," Brody grasped her arm. "The other girls," indicating Miss McCool and Miss Dean, who, each holding to one of Tancel's arms, were beginning the ascent, "are starting up. We can't let them leave us behind."

"Dr. Lipscomb," Miss Tredkin turned an appealing face to the conductor, "you don't really think it's safe, do you?"

"Assuredly, Miss Tredkin, no danger at all. And the view from the top is one of the grandest in Mexico."

She stood for a moment in indecision, her lower lip held firmly between her teeth, "I guess I'll go part way up."

"Thata girl!" one of Brody's hands encircled her arm, "let's go!"

Slowly, with frequent pauses for breath, the party climbed upward.

Miss McCool, Miss Dean and Tancel were the first to gain the top, followed by Colonel Enloe and Rennert, Mr. and Mrs. Earp, Dr. Lipscomb and Professor Bymaster.

From that height the ancient City of the Gods and the surrounding valley lay before their eyes—a breathtaking panorama. To the north the Pyramid of the Moon, faintly discernible to the south the outlines of the Temple of Quetzalcoatl. On all sides, stretching away to the gray-blue mountains, a checkerboard of brown and green, dotted with maguey plants. They were more than human, lifted by human handiwork toward the sun in a sky of blue silk.

"Oh, isn't it perfectly gorgeous!" Miss McCool broke the spell and they were again a group of tourists on a truncated pyramid.

"Hello, folks, we made it!" Miss Tredkin, propelled by Brady's hand, stepped upon the top. Her face was flushed and her breath came in short quick gasps, but a poorly suppressed thrill of excitement was in her thin voice. "Thank you so much, Mr. Brody, for helping me."

"Where are the Willises?" Dr. Lipscomb asked, looking over his little flock.

Earp laughed. "They gave it up and stopped after the first flight of steps. She said that his heart wouldn't stand the climb. I tried to tell the wife she ought to stay down there, too, but she wouldn't do it, so I had to haul her up."

"Ah, Ed, you know you wouldn't have wanted to come if I hadn't, would you?" Mrs. Earp lisped, her blue eyes gazing up into her husband's.

"Rats!" the exclamation, *sotto voce*, came, Rennert thought as he quickly suppressed a smile, from one of the Texas school teachers.

"This pyramid," Dr. Lipscomb said in a loud voice, "is the pyramid of the Sun, the largest at Teotihuacan. This old city was the capital of the Toltecs, who lived here long before the Aztecs came to the Valley of Mexico. In front of you is the famous Roadway of the Dead—"

"Want to use these?" Colonel Enloe, at Rennert's side, proffered a pair of field glasses.

"Thanks." Rennert took them, gazed at the magnificent sweep of the Roadway, the long rows of tombs upon either side.

For an instant he forgot the present and thought of that scene as he had once looked upon it, years before. That was on his second visit to Mexico. He had come alone and had stood for hours upon this summit, drenched in moonlight, while his mind, drunk with the unearthly beauty of it, had played with fanciful thoughts of what this old city must have looked like in the days of its full glory, what it would look like now if the kings and priests were to emerge in grandeur from those old tombs and ascend those steps in ghostly procession. . . .

"The Toltecs attained a high degree of civilization, as you can see by these ruins," Dr. Lipscomb's voice continued. "Their tutelary deity was Quetzalcoatl, the famous Fair God. According to the legends he came to them from the East, taught them the arts of civilization, then went away again, promising to return—"

Rennert took the field glasses from his eyes, passed them to Mrs. Earp.

"Oh, Mr. Rennert, thank you so much!"

Her pudgy little fingers, upon which a wedding ring of tarnished gold was almost lost to sight in the folds of soft white flesh, fumbled with the glasses.

"Ed, I can't make these little screws and things work. I can't see a thing."

"Here, let me show you." Earp's deft fingers adjusted the glasses, held them to her eyes. "How's that?"

"Oh, that's fine. I can see everything now."

"Now," Dr. Lipscomb said, "we will go down and visit the Temple of Quetzalcoatl. Be sure to notice the carved serpents' heads and the traces of paint still visible. Now, Miss Tredkin, don't look down like that, just take it slowly and don't think how high up you are. If you feel dizzy just hold onto Mr. Brody's arm."

The descent accomplished, they made their way back toward the cars. While the rest stopped to buy clay figurines from a woman and two small children, Rennert found himself walking beside Colonel Enloe.

"A great sight, isn't it, Rennert," Enloe indicated the pyramid with a motion of the head. "Entirely different from the pyramids of Egypt. Rather reminds me of the terraced hillsides of the Philippines. You've seen them?"

"No, I haven't."

"I was stationed out there for five years."

"You are retired from the army now, aren't you, Colonel?"

"Yes, have been for three years now. Making my home with my daughter—I'm a widower, you know—and taking things easy, doing a bit of traveling. Get kind of restless, though, sometimes. Not used to this soft life yet. Have a cigar?"

He drew a thin wooden box from his pocket and proffered it. Rennert took one and accepted a light from Enloe.

"Where are you from, Rennert?" the latter asked, as they strolled on.

Rennert repeated his story.

"Ever do any hunting, Rennert?" Enloe asked.

"A little."

"Wish you'd come down sooner and we'd have gone out in the mountains for a few days. They say these hills are full of deer. I suppose you're going back with us day after tomorrow?"

"Yes."

"We should have gotten together sooner. Well, here are the cars. Say, why don't you stop by my room sometime? We'll have a drink together."

"Thanks, I'll do that."

The others joined them then. They were conducted by Dr. Lipscomb with abrupt efficiency through the quadrangle of the Temple of Quetalcoatl; they gazed dutifully at the plumed serpents; they descended far underground into passages through buried temples. Then they were in the cars again, being whirled over dusty plains toward Mexico City.

Rennert sat on the rear seat with Miss Tredkin and Brody. Professor Bymaster occupied the front seat.

The experiences of the morning seemed to have excited the professor, for he grew talkative and gazed from side to side, commenting on the landscape.

"Those pyramids were a most impressive sight and I understand that each altar and temple is placed so that the rays of the sun will strike a particular portion on a certain day in a given season. Had you ever realized, Miss Tredkin, the full significance of the astronomical knowledge of these peoples?"

Miss Tredkin, sitting rigid beside Mr. Brody, started at the mention of her name, looked uncertainly at the speaker, as if trying to decide what answer was expected of her. Before she had made up her mind, Dr. Bymaster was off on another track.

"The country around here is devoted almost entirely to maguey plantations. Those are magueys over there on your right, Miss Tredkin—no, no, on your right. That plant with the tall green leaves. The maguey serves a great number of uses here in Mexico, but the principal use is to make pulque, the national drink. Nearly a million acres of agricultural land are devoted to the raising of the maguey. It gives employment to a million and a half people and pays ten million pesos in taxes. Had you realized, Miss Tredkin, the full extent of this industry? Probably not—"

Miss Tredkin's back grew straighter and her chin was set at a determined angle.

"Yes, Professor Bymaster, I realized that. I once read a paper on the evil grip which pulque has on the Mexican people to our unit of the W.C.T.U. back in Wichita. I, you know, am from Kansas and our state has always been dry. The liquor interests have done their best to break down our resistance, but in vain. The women of Kansas stand foursquare behind the Volstead Act."

She paused, took a deep breath and continued in a slightly lower voice.

"When I see men, American men, down here in Mexico, reeling in the streets and through hotel lobbies under the influence of drink, forgetful of their manhood and of the ties which bind them to their loved ones at home, I say 'Thank God for Kansas!'"

Her lips closed firmly and she sank back in her seat.

Silence—the heavy silence of a Mexican countryside at noon—fell over them.

Rennert cast a sideways glance at Brody. The big man was slumped down in his seat, his eyes fixed on the floor of the car. One hand was running a handkerchief over his flushed face.

"Your book, Dr. Bymaster," Rennert grabbed the first thought which came to his mind, "how is it progressing?

"Excellently. I am anxious to return to the United States and complete my chapter on Mexico."

"What is the scope of your book?"

"It is to be an economic survey of our modern world, with especial emphasis on the undeveloped resources in backward countries, such as Mexico."

He began a summary of the book. When they arrived at the hotel in Mexico City, he had reached chapter four—"The Hinterland of China."

They got out of the car—Professor Bymaster with a far-away look in his eyes; Miss Tredkin, silent and square-chinned; Brody, humbly polite and red of face as he helped her from the car; Rennert, an amused twinkle (discernible only to one who knew him well) deep in his eyes.

The rest of the party were scattering.

In the lobby an insignificant-looking, dark-eyed man exchanged glances with Rennert and, in a few moments, followed him to his room.

Rennert admitted him at his knock, drew him inside.

"You followed Argudin today?"

"Yes, I followed him all day. He got up at ten, ate breakfast, walked through the Alameda, returned to the hotel, played at cards all the afternoon. Now he is in his room."

"Who did he play cards with?"

"Three men who stay here at the hotel. I have here their names." He handed Rennert a slip of paper.

Rennert glanced at it, then looked up. "Did Argudin," he asked, "win any money?"

"Yes, *mucho*." A gesture of upraised palms and a decided nod of the head.

Rennert smiled and likewise nodded.

"You have more orders, Mr. Rennert?"

"No, not tonight."

"Tomorrow, yes?"

"Tomorrow, yes."

And that day, although he did not then know it, Rennert had come across his first indication of the truth.

11
SEARCH

MEXICAN MORNINGS have often been compared with cold heady wine.

That, Rennert thought as he walked briskly through the Alameda, expressed it exactly. Cold, heady wine.

The exercise sent the blood pulsing through his veins and aided, in a measure, in relieving the feeling of despondency into which he was beginning to fall. Their last day in Mexico City. Day after tomorrow they would cross the border. Inspector Miles would be there waiting for them, with handcuffs. He must then point to one of these people with whom he had been associated for the past few days and say: "This person is guilty." There must be no doubt, no lack of proof.

And who was this person? Willis? Rennert's stride slowed down. Again he went over Willis' actions and words since he had joined the party. Except for the evidence of a clerk in San Antonio that Willis, or someone answering closely his description, had bought a pair of black silk stockings the day of Payne's murder and for the quite evident agitation of both the Willises that day in Sanborn's when the subject of the murder had been brought up, there was nothing to connect the St. Louis jeweler with this business. If nothing more incriminating showed up during these two days, would he be justified in ordering Willis' arrest? Yes, he told himself again, he would. If there were any explanation for the purchase of those stockings Willis should give it.

Several times Rennert had been on the point of informing Willis of his identity and demanding pointblank that he answer his accusation. Each time he had demurred. If the man were guilty such an action would warn him, enable him to cover his tracks and possibly escape, whereas if he continued confident of his immunity from suspicion and ignorant of Rennert's presence in the party some clew inadvertently overlooked might prove his undoing. If Willis were innocent and could prove his innocence Rennert's incognito would in all probability be lost and the true criminal put on his guard.

Dr. Lipscomb's party had gone to Cuernavaca and Taxco early that morning. Rennert, seeing them off, had noted that three had remained in Mexico City. Mrs. Rankin, Miss Dean and Argudin.

Rennert at the last moment had changed his mind and decided to remain in the capital, conducting himself a search of the rooms of the absent tourists instead of intrusting this task to one of the Mexican secret service operatives, as he had first planned.

The hotel manager (a fat, voluble Frenchman) when interviewed in his office proved courteous to the point of obsequiousness. It had been arranged, he said, that his distinguished guest, Mr. Rennert, was to be allowed, nay aided, to enter as he wished the rooms of the members of Dr. Lipscomb's party. There followed many low-voiced conferences with various employees, all of whom fell in with the prevailing atmosphere of conspiracy. As Rennert walked across the lobby, ascended to the fifth floor on the elevator and emerged into the hall with an excited young man at his elbow, he felt that he should be wearing a long black cape or twirling a pair of mustachios.

The excited young man quickly dispersed a little group of chattering maids who had gathered in one end of the hall and informed Rennert with a grandiloquent gesture that he might proceed. The *señora* in room 559 and the *señorita* in 554 had not yet gone out. The other rooms were empty. He drew from a pocket a key, handed it to Rennert. The *señor* desired his aid, yes? Rennert regretted it very, very much, but he did not desire his aid. With Rennert's permission, then, the young man would withdraw.

Dr. Lipscomb's party occupied one wing of the floor. On Rennert's right were four double rooms which faced the street. These (he consulted a memorandum) were occupied by Mr. and Mrs.

Willis, by Miss Dean and Miss McCool, by Brody and Enloe and by Mr. and Mrs. Earp. On his left, facing the court, were six single rooms, occupied by Argudin, Bymaster, Tancel, Dr. Lipscomb (in the center, as it were, of his flock), Miss Tredkin and Mrs. Rankin.

Rennert inserted the pass key into the lock of the Willises' room and entered.

It was a large apartment and faced the east. The French windows opening on the little railed balcony were closed. Rennert threw them open and stood looking about him.

As he expected, everything was neatly in order, from the closed drawers of the wardrobe trunk in the corner to the toilet articles on the dresser. Rennert drew a chair in front of the trunk and with practiced fingers examined its contents. He found nothing to interest him. He got up and walked to the clothes closet, where he glanced briefly at several letters in the inner pocket of one of Willis' suits and at the tailor's label. He tried the dresser next. From the upper left-hand drawer he took out half a dozen pairs of silk stockings and looked at them thoughtfully. They were new and still bore the price tags, those of a Mexico City department store. They were of various shades of gray. He put them back in the drawer and went hastily through the contents of the other drawers. From each of them, as he opened it, arose the sweet, pungent odor of mothballs. He examined the luggage—two black gladstones upon a stand near the window. They were empty and each bore the little round tag which identified it as belonging to the Inter-America Tours party. He felt the lining and tapped the bottoms, then put them back in their places. He removed the bedclothes and mattresses on the twin beds, tossed them back.

Then he went out and locked the door behind him.

He stood for a few moments and let the fresh air from the window drain the faintly sour smell of stale cigar smoke and the sundry undeniably masculine odors from the room occupied by Colonel Enloe and Mr. Brody.

On a table by the side of one of the twin beds stood an empty bottle of Highland Queen and two glasses. A deck of cards lay face upwards. Poker chips covered the rest of the surface of the table.

Rennert, as he proceeded to subject the room to a minute scrutiny, observed the imprint of the two personalities of the men who occupied it. Colonel Enloe's carefully pressed suits were arranged in a scrupulously exact row along one side of the closet. His shoes, black or dark tan and polished to a mirror-like brightness, stood beneath them. In the dresser drawers appropriated by him, his shirts, underwear, handkerchiefs and socks were in neat piles. Brody's belongings were everywhere, as if he had stood in the center of the room and tossed them from him at random. The two blue serge suits which hung askew on hangers in the closet were badly in need of pressing. His other clothing had not been removed from the battered satchel and gladstone which stood open upon the stand.

Rennert examined the contents of the closet first. The pockets of Colonel Enloe's clothing contained nothing. Hanging from a nail behind them was a leather holster. Rennert carried it to the light. It held a Colt automatic—a .45. Rennert examined it, balanced it in his hand. He returned it to its holster and hung the holster on the nail in the closet again.

He ran a hand along the shelf at the end of the closet, felt of something with his fingers, drew it down. His body stiffened involuntarily. Walking hurriedly from the semi-darkness of the closet, he carried the coiled object to the light, stared at it curiously.

It was about eight feet of rope, soft pliable cotton rope, perhaps a fourth of an inch in diameter. It was obviously new.

Rennert stood for a long time, drawing the soft strand through his fingers, thinking hard. His face was set and his eyes were narrowed as he walked slowly back to the closet and returned the rope to the shelf.

Young Payne in that San Antonio morgue. The undertaker had done his work by the time Rennert had arrived, of course. But he remembered the faces of other men who had died by strangulation. . . .

To shut out the picture he set about the rest of his task with vigor. He took several letters from Brody's pockets, read them carefully before returning them. He examined carefully the contents of the dresser and of the luggage. Attached to each piece of the latter was a round red tag. A steamer trunk, bearing Colonel Enloe's initials, was locked. A deft movement with a small instrument which Rennert took from his pocket and the lock flew open. He examined the contents with swift thoroughness, but found nothing to interest him. He took the beds next, ransacked them. Then the bathroom. From the top shelf of the medicine closet he took down a small bottle of (he examined the label, pulled out the cork and sniffed the contents) brown hair dye. He regarded it speculatively, turned it round and round in his fingers. (Sandy-colored hair, he thought, with just a touch of gray at the temples. Reddish-brown hair, thin at the crown of the head. A few gray streaks here and there.) He put the bottle back on the shelf and went into the other room.

He surveyed his surroundings for some time, then knelt down and threw back the dark green rug. He pulled the bed away from the wall, rolled up the other half of the rug. He got to his feet, dusted off the knees of his trousers and left the room, cursing himself for having delayed so long this examination.

The room at the end of the corridor, occupied by the Earps, presented a scene of confusion equal to that of the one which Rennert had just left. On the chairs and over the foot of the beds were strewn various articles of clothing—a pair of gray trousers, pajamas, lingerie which had probably cost a great deal of money at one time. Rennert inspected the clothing in the closet—two suits bearing the label of a Chicago tailor, the pockets of which contained nothing except a fountain pen; a row of expensive-looking silk dresses, most of them showing signs of wear, and with labels of famous makers in New York and Paris; a cluttered shelf of shoes.

The luggage (a black steamer trunk, a worn hat box with the initials MJE and an obviously new suitcase) was unlocked and contained nothing except a few odds and ends—soiled handkerchiefs, a package of cigarettes, a pocket-size Spanish-English dictionary, an old letter addressed in a feminine hand to Mrs. Edward Earp at a street address in Chicago and containing (Rennert found when he opened it) a lengthy, exclamatory account of the Olympic Games in Los Angeles, which some friend of Mrs. Earp's was attending. There was a reference to mutual acquaintances in a business office. Rennert noted that the suitcase did not bear one of the little round tags.

He turned his attention to the dresser but found nothing to interest him except a small automatic revolver—a Smith & Wesson .38—and several boxes of shells, one of them blanks. He went over the rest of the room in a rather perfunctory manner, locked the door and crossed the hall.

Facing him were the doors of Mrs. Rankin's and Miss Tredkin's rooms. He passed them and entered Dr. Lipscomb's chamber.

His procedure here was similar to that which he had followed in the other rooms. The conductor's clothing (confined, Rennert noted, to the barest necessities) was in order; his luggage, all tagged, empty and carefully arranged in a row on the closet shelf. Rennert found nothing to interest him until he had finished. Then he took the brief case from the top of the dresser and sat down in the armchair, lighted a cigarette and proceeded to examine the contents. It was full of letters and papers and Rennert spent almost half an hour at his task. At last he closed the case, got up and laid it on the dresser.

Tancel's room was easily searched. The young man had brought only a worn gladstone and a small satchel. They were tagged and stood open upon a stand by the window. His clothing had not been removed. Rennert examined the gladstone, then turned his attention to the satchel. When his fingers reached the bottom, he paused and examined the outside of the bag. Carrying it to the bed, he removed the contents and subjected it to a close scrutiny. He was smiling as he manipulated a little catch and the false bottom slid out of place, revealing a space of about an inch beneath. Rennert stood for a moment, thinking, before he replaced the false bottom, arranged the clothes as he had found them and put the satchel on the stand.

In three minutes he had gone over the rest of Tancel's room and was in the adjoining one. His examination of Professor Bymaster's effects was conducted with swift thoroughness, but he did not fail to notice that the steamer trunk under the bed did not bear the same round red label as the other luggage.

The last room on this side of the corridor was occupied by Argudin. Rennert, when he had closed the door behind him, stood for a moment and sniffed. Then, with a grimace of distaste, he crossed the room and threw open the window. The breeze blew several playing cards from the table. Rennert picked them up, glanced at them and slipped one into his pocket. He went to the dresser where a small bottle and a camel's hair brush held his attention for a moment. He put them down suddenly and stared thoughtfully at a pair of false teeth which lay upon the top of the dresser. An upper and a lower plate. Rennert turned them over in his fingers. They had obviously never been used. He laid them down and turned to the three pieces of luggage which stood upon the rack. A small steamer trunk, a brown gladstone and a black satchel. Attached to the handles of all of them were the round red tags of the Inter-America Tours. Rennert laid the steamer trunk upon the floor in front of him. It was locked. Again he took from his pocket the small instrument, knelt down and applied it to the lock. . . .

"If you prefer," a low voice spoke from the doorway, "you may make use of my key."

12
BUTTONED FOILS

RENNERT GOT UP DELIBERATELY, brushed the knees of his trousers and turned to face Argudin.

"Thank you," he said evenly, "if you will be so kind."

Argudin, his white firm-looking teeth flashing in a smile, stepped forward. He drew from his pocket key-ring, handed it to Rennert.

"The small thin key will open the trunk," he said. "The long round one the gladstone. The other is, I believe, unlocked." He walked past Rennert, glanced at the black satchel. "Yes, it is unlocked." He drew out a package of cigarettes, proffered them. "Smoke? No? You doubtless prefer an American brand. I regret exceedingly that I have only the Mexican kind. I believe, you see, in conforming to the customs of the country in which I happen to be. When I am in Mexico, I smoke Mexican cigarettes. You doubtless find them a trifle strong—and sweet. Most Americans do at first. If I had known that I was to have the pleasure of a visit from Mr.—ah, yes, Rennert—I should have supplied myself. The next time, yes. But," his small, slender hands went upward in a gesture, "I delay you from your work. Please proceed. I trust that I do not disturb you if I remain in the room."

He sauntered to the window, where he stood with his back turned, blowing slow smoke rings outward over the court.

Rennert stood for a moment, watching him, then knelt upon the floor again and opened the steamer trunk. His practiced fingers went through the contents swiftly. He closed and locked it,

82

replaced it upon the rack. He did the same with the gladstone and the satchel. He arose.

"That is all, Mr. Argudin."

The other turned from the window.

"Have you noticed," he asked, "what a magnificent view of Chapultepec Castle one obtains from this window? The cliffs rise straight upward above the tops of the *ahuehuete* trees under which Montezuma used to walk. But, of course, you have seen Chapultepec before, Mr. Rennert. You have finished? Yes? Will you not be seated? This is the first time I have had the pleasure of a visit from you."

His dark, petal-shaped eyes met Rennert's as the latter handed him the ring of keys.

"Many thanks, Mr. Rennert. You should have asked for them and saved yourself this trouble. Ah, yes, be seated."

Rennert sat down, crossed his legs and lit a cigarette. The little room was suddenly still, muffled (the odd thought came to him) by layer upon layer of dark smooth silk. The smoke of the two cigarettes rose in tiny, pencil-like lines, to splay outward into the spiral volutes of twin Ionic capitals as it touched the soft enveloping silk. . . .

"You were looking for something, Mr. Rennert," Argudin's voice was as expressionless as his stare as his eyes met Rennert's. "I trust that you did not find it?"

"No, Mr. Argudin, I did not find what I was looking for."

"Ah," the black eyebrows rose, "but you found something else?"

Rennert continued to look thoughtfully at Argudin. (His inflection of those words had been unintentional, yet this dark-eyed man had caught the meaning which lay behind them.)

"I found," he said, "several things."

"In your line?" The pupils of Argudin's eyes contracted a little.

"Perhaps I should explain what my line is?"

A slender white hand waved aside the suggestion.

"It is not necessary, Mr. Rennert. I think we understand each other."

His eyes remained on Rennert's face, waiting.

"No," Rennert said, "I found nothing in my line." His eyes were fixed on the pearl-white teeth which the other's set smile made visible. "May I ask how you knew?"

Argudin laughed. It was a soft laugh, its pleasantness drawn by a faint metallic quality.

"Simple, Mr. Rennert. The men whom your government chooses for such little—ah, investigations, shall we say?—are of a distressing, tiresome sameness. I refer, of course, to their appearance and manner."

Rennert's smile was impersonal.

"You have had experience with us, then, Mr. Argudin?"

"Really, Mr. Rennert," Argudin continued to smile as his long, well manicured fingers crushed a cigarette into the ashtray, "you lose discretion. Shall we not keep the buttons upon our foils?"

"Certainly," Rennert's laugh was pleasant, "my error. But you were about to explain how you knew."

"Ah, yes. One hears of many, many little games little schemes for avoiding the eyes of Cerberus—I see you understand me, Mr. Rennert. My pleasure in knowing you is increased. It is not often that one finds comprehension of classical allusions in men of your calling. I do my best to avoid them. They give one, you know, the reputation of being—how do you say it? A snob? Yes, a snob. The Spanish has the same word, but I was not certain whether they had appropriated it from the English or from the French. I was unfortunate in my university education, altogether in the classics. So impractical—"

"You were explaining how you knew."

"But yes," Argudin's thin shoulders rose in a deprecative shrug, "we Latins have the unfortunate habit of straying from the point, we love to ramble aimlessly in our conversation, to savor the attractions of the little bypaths of talk. The straight broad highway of you Nordics grows tiresome to us. But I was saying that one hears these rumors of ingenious little games. In the small hotel in San Antonio where a certain party of tourists stayed one night a man is murdered. One hears that he was seeking another man who had developed a new little scheme. Suddenly Mr. Rennert appears in

Mexico City, joins Dr. Lipscomb's select travel party. Mr. Rennert is, you will pardon me the compliment which I pay you, most certainly not a tourist. I remember that it was Dr. Lipscomb's party which stayed in that little hotel in San Antonio where a man was murdered and I say to myself— But, is there any need for me to tell you what I say to myself, Mr. Rennert?"

"None at all, Mr. Argudin. Does our—shall I say tacit agreement—permit you to tell me if any other person in this party suspects my identity?"

"I do not know, Mr. Rennert." Argudin's face was impassive as he selected another cigarette. "I do not inquire too closely into the secrets of my fellow travelers. It might not be for me altogether—safe."

Rennert uncrossed his knees and sat erect in the chair. His face was thoughtful.

"I should appreciate it, Mr. Argudin, if you pursued that policy with regard to myself."

Argudin's eyes were steady as they met Rennert's over the tiny flame of the match which he was holding to his cigarette.

"Reciprocity?" he asked softly.

Rennert nodded. "Yes. I likewise do not inquire too closely into the secrets of my fellow travelers—as long as they do not concern me."

Argudin tossed the match into the tray.

"Very well, Mr. Rennert. We understand each other."

Rennert got to his feet. He took from his pocket a playing card, placed it upon the table.

"A proof," he said, smiling, "of my good intentions."

Argudin's face did not alter. "Thank you, Mr. Rennert," he said, rising and giving his head a slight inclination. And, as Rennert opened the door, he asked:

"We are to have the pleasure of your company on our return trip, Mr. Rennert?"

"Yes," Rennert's eyes met his, "I shall be present on the return trip."

He stepped into the corridor and closed the door behind him.

For perhaps five minutes Argudin stood in the center of the room without moving. Then he went softly to the door, opened it and looked up and down the corridor. He closed the door, locked it and came back into the room. He took from the top of the dresser the pair of white false teeth and examined them. Humming softly to himself he carried them into the bathroom and put them on the top shelf of the medicine cabinet. Then he went into the bedroom and stood at the window. He tossed the butt of his cigarette into the courtyard below, watched it spin downward.

Then, as he stood gazing over the flat roofs toward Chapultepec, he drew a handkerchief from the breast pocket of his coat and passed it over his forehead, where little beads of perspiration had stood.

13
ESCAPE

MISS DEAN SAT, one leg curled up under her, in a big leather chair.

The reading room was in the semi-darkness of late afternoon and the reading lamp behind her sent its rays full upon her hair, melting and fusing the copper into a reddish glow. Her head was bent over a gaudily jacketed book.

In a few minutes she yawned, closed the book and glanced in Rennert's direction. She straightened her posture and smiled.

"Won't you come over here and talk to me?" she asked.

He arose, moved his chair to her side.

"I know you'd rather sit over there by yourself than talk to me," she said abruptly, turning her eyes to his face. They were dark brown eyes with a peculiar pin-point of green in the pupils. They lent interest to an otherwise uninteresting face. "But," she continued, smiling faintly, "it's what you get for joining a tour. You have to talk to people, listen to their confidences. I expect you have listened to a lot of them in the last few days."

"A few, yes."

"You missed your calling, Mr. Rennert," she said suddenly.

"My calling?"

"Yes, you should have been a priest, a father confessor. You have such kind friendly eyes that everyone would feel free to confide their troubles to you."

Rennert laughed. "Thank you, Miss Dean. I have always felt, though, that that is a calling which should be reserved for those

87

who can give advice without feeling too keenly the sufferings of others. Advice, you know, should be impersonal—if it is worthwhile."

"That's true." Her eyes wandered to the profusely decorated pillar behind his head. "Do you have a cigarette?"

He took out a package, watched her fingers tremble slightly as she accepted a cigarette. He struck a match and held it out.

Soft wings brushed between their faces, fanning the still air. The tiny flame flickered, was gone.

"What was that?" there was a catch of fright in her voice.

Rennert watched fascinated as a huge black butterfly circled slowly toward the ceiling.

"Just one of those big black butterflies that one sees late in the afternoon in Mexico."

"It scared me—it was so sudden."

Rennert smiled. "Yes, their color and peculiar markings and their sudden swoop out of the darkness are rather unnerving. The natives fear them."

"Fear them?"

"Yes," Rennert struck another match and held it to the end of her cigarette, "they say that it is an omen of death."

"They have lots of these superstitions down here, don't they?" The girl drew contentedly upon the cigarette.

"Yes, they fear these omens more than death itself. Death is explicable, the omens are not."

She smoked for a moment in silence, then laughed and pointed to the book upon her lap.

"The butterfly must have known what I was reading."

Rennert, growing accustomed to the unexpected veerings of her talk, glanced at the book.

"*Murder Comes Uninvited.* You are a murder story fan, Miss Dean?"

"Yes. This is one of those murder party ones, where they pretend that one of the guests has been murdered. Then it is discovered that it was an actual murder."

"Ingenious," Rennert laughed.

"Yes, too ingenious, I'm afraid. But that's one reason I like murder stories. They're so unreal, not like the kind you read about in the newspapers. Miss Tredkin told me the other day that I shouldn't read so many of them, that they would make me morbid. I didn't try to explain to her the real reason why I read them. I don't think she would have understood."

"No, I don't think that Miss Tredkin understands escape."

"Escape?" she shot him a quick glance. "How did you know?"

"Most people do read them for that reason, Miss Dean. They are just one of the many avenues of escape from the realities of life. They keep one from thinking about—other things."

She let the smoke trickle slowly from her mouth, watched it through half-closed eyes as it writhed upward in the still air.

"Such as what one doesn't have," she murmured as if to herself. "I didn't go with the others to Cuernavaca today," she said, looking at Rennert.

"So I notice."

"I told them that I wanted to do some shopping." She flicked the ash from her cigarette into a tray. "I lied, of course."

Rennert remained silent.

"They'll be back in a few minutes," she went on, "and I'll have to start my act. I'm just resting and being myself for a few minutes. I'll be expected to be the life of the party tonight." She laughed dryly. "I suppose I might as well make the most of it, though. I'll be teaching school in a small town in Texas this time next year."

"While Miss McCool—" Rennert said softly.

"Will have what she wants. Money usually gets it and Cuernavaca, they say, is a romantic place. Lindbergh and Anne had their courtship there, you know. Even in Cuernavaca, though, one would be foolish to allow competition."

She glanced down into the lobby, crushed her cigarette into the tray and turned to Rennert.

"Here they come. You'll forget this little—ah, eruption of mine, won't you?"

"Yes," he arose and stood, hands in pockets, looking down at her. "There is no end to the supply of murder stories, if that is any consolation."

She laughed. "Thanks, Mr. Rennert."

"Ah, there's our little Gertie!" Miss McCool's happy, high-pitched voice made them turn around. Arm in arm, she and Tancel were advancing across the floor. "You missed the most wonderful trip, dearie!"

"Banana trees and swimming pools and cathedrals and mountains and everything," Tancel chimed in.

"Aw, hell, I've seen those things until I'm sick of 'em." Miss Dean stretched herself lazily. "What about a drink before dinner?"

Rennert made his departure unnoticed.

14
A HOUSE IN SAN ANGEL

Dusk—the quick, shroudlike Mexican dusk—was falling as Rennert walked slowly through the Alameda.

The flaring gasoline torches lit a feverishly unreal scene of Dantesque phantasmagoria, viewed in the shifting glass of a kaleidoscope. The branches of the trees seemed to writhe in agony and the pungent odor of frying fat in charcoal braziers pricked his nostrils. A Ferris-wheel was a gigantic, many-headed serpent with interminable gaping mouths and flashing feathers, like the stone serpents on Toltec temples.

The scene fitted oddly Rennert's mood. He felt, as he often felt when he saw the sharp outlines of the mountains change into dark, shapeless, antediluvian creatures hemming in the valley, a frantic, overpowering sense of panic rising from primitive, atavistic depths within him. So, he had often thought, must his forebears have felt when they huddled in the recesses of a cave and stared across a protecting fire at the unguessed terrors of the darkness beyond. Thus had ogres come into being and the strange gods whose broken images underlay this valley.

A man with a white skin, he told himself, had no business thinking in this country. Tomorrow he was leaving; the next day he would cross the border.

The border became to his mind a far-away, yet sharply defined goal, the end of this grim bewildering chase. For one or two of the things which he had seen that afternoon in those hotel rooms bewildered him, upset his carefully made estimates of the people who were living in them for a short, rapidly ending time. For the first time a doubt assailed him. When he and this little group of individuals crossed the thin line of water that was the Rio Grande and paused briefly before going their separate ways—when that time came, must he admit failure? Must he watch them pass out of his sight, bid them good-by and still not know which one of them—

At the entrance of the hotel he came face to face with Mrs. Rankin.

The dark brim of her hat and the upturned collar of her coat made her old face look pale and curiously fragile. In one hand she carried a small bag of black leather.

She smiled as Rennert paused and removed his hat.

"Good evening, Mrs. Rankin."

"Good evening, Mr. Rennert."

The night air was cold on Rennert's bare head and he put on his hat again.

"Leaving, Mrs. Rankin?"

"Yes," her bright eyes were on his face, "for a time."

She drew her coat about her with one hand and stood for a moment looking at him.

"Would you be gallant enough," she asked, "to accompany me?"

"With pleasure, Mrs. Rankin."

He took the little bag from her hand and, at her direction, hailed a taxicab. She gave the destination to the driver. It was a street number in the little suburb of San Angel.

They sat for a few minutes in silence, each upright in the impersonal plush covering of the rear seat. The wind from the mountains was chill as it whipped their faces. The electric lights of the Paseo de la Reforma lined the darkness. Rennert gazed at a pinpoint of light far above him to his right, speculated idly whether it was from a corner of Chapultepec Castle or a distant star. . . .

"You are wondering where we are going," Mrs. Rankin's bell-like voice fell softly on his ears.

Rennert did not reply. (Chapultepec lay behind them, it must be a star.)

"Out at San Angel," Mrs. Rankin said, "there is a house."

(Her face was turned from him, as if she too were looking at that little light.)

"It is a small house, with flowers in the patio and bougainvillea on the walls. I lived three years in that house."

They had left the Pasco. Darkness lay now between the rectangular glows from doors and windows of houses. The lights of the car were faint candle-flares in space.

"Love," Mrs. Rankin continued, "came to me late in my life. I was past forty and had settled into the calm backwaters of life. He was an engineer, back from Mexico for a short stay in the States. He was even older than I and knew, too, the quiet currents of existence. It was the same old story."

(Bells in weather-beaten old churches, Rennert thought, get that mellow sound from the years.)

"We loved, were married and came to Mexico to live. Together we arranged this house in San Angel. It was for ourselves alone, like a patio hidden behind high walls. Three years—and he died."

They were being carried straight into the black mountains, like chips borne on a wave to dash against the insensate granite of cliffs.

"He had lived long here in Mexico," Mrs. Rankin's straight back did not relax its rigid poise, "and knew and loved her people. He used to say that here the veil between the living and the dead is thinner than in other places. He believed many of these strange old stories one hears down here. I used to listen to him without voicing my disbelief. In time I began to wonder—about things. These people are so calm in their confidence. Once he said that if one of us died before the other, we would have a tryst in this house on the Night of the Dead. Where we had lived together. I thought at the time that he was joking. Now I do not know."

A tiny furry creature ran into the road, stood for an instant blinded by the glare of the headlights, dashed back into the darkness.

Mrs. Rankin sat for a long time motionless. The car turned into the narrow streets of San Angel and the faint, pervasive scent of flowers seemed to envelop them.

"I left the house with an old servant woman," Mrs. Rankin said, her voice barely audible now; "his room is as he left it. Once a year, on the Night of the Dead, I come back here, sleep in his bed. He has not yet come back, but I feel somehow," a street lamp shone on her tightly clenched, black gloved hands, "that each time he is nearer to me. Each year I hope that he will come. Perhaps, I tell myself, it will be tonight."

The car drew up in front of a little iron gate set in a high stone wall almost hidden by masses of bougainvillea.

"This is the house," Mrs. Rankin said.

They got out.

At the gate she turned and extended a hand to Rennert. He saw the smile on her face and the brightness of her eyes as she said:

"Good-by—and may you sleep better for having listened to a silly old woman."

15
COLONEL ENLOE DRESSES

R<small>ENNERT'S TELEPHONE</small> rang softly. (Was it his imagination, he had often asked himself, or do Mexican telephones have a subdued, restrained quality in their ring?)

Colonel Enloe's voice came to him over the wire.

"Going to Lipscomb's dinner party tonight, Rennert? What about coming by the room for a few minutes? We'll have a drink before we go down."

Rennert assented, and hung up the receiver.

He hastily finished his toilet and put on his coat. He felt curiously alert as he went down the stairs and knocked at the door of Enloe's room. The Smith & Wesson revolver in his hip pocket was hard and reassuring.

The colonel, in undershirt and trousers, opened the door.

"Come in, come in," he stepped aside. "Make yourself at home."

Rennert entered and sat down.

"I thought," Enloe said, "that this would probably be a dry party tonight and that we'd better have a shot before we go."

He busied himself with siphon and a bottle.

"Good idea," Rennert said. His eyes were fixed idly on Enloe's straight pink shoulders and broad chest. Down the upper part of his left arm ran a long narrow scar.

Colonel Enloe handed him a glass and sat on the edge of the bed.

"Here's how!" he said. He drained his glass at one gulp and set it on the table.

95

"Where's Brody?" Rennert asked, his eyes on the whisky which remained in the bottom of his glass. Enloe, engaged in removing the tinfoil from a cigar, laughed.

"The damn fool is out with that old maid from Kansas," he said. "She's helping him buy some Mexican clothes for his kids."

He looked up, met Rennert's eyes, and laughed again.

"There's no fool," he said, "like an old fool. Help yourself to a cigar." He shoved forward a box. Rennert took one, unwrapped it slowly.

"Did you and Brody know each other before you came down here?" he asked, flipping the wrapper into the cuspidor beside the bed.

"No, I met him on the train coming down. He's from the same part of the country that I am and we have some mutual friends at Fort Sill. Brody looked like the best bet in this bunch, so I tied up with him. He's a good fellow, all right, but like a kid with a new toy with all this money."

Rennert lit his cigar. "Oil, isn't it?"

"Yes, he's got a lot of land out in West Texas—used to be ranch land. They struck oil on it last year and so Brody has a lot of money on his hands and nothing to do except spend it. He's a widower, you know."

Enloe got up and walked to the dresser.

"Pardon me," he said, "and I'll go ahead dressing. Help yourself to the whisky."

"So this is our last night in Mexico," Rennert said in a moment.

"Yes," Enloe's back was turned as he took a shirt from a drawer. "We leave in the morning. Everything packed?"

"Not yet."

Silence fell between them.

"By the way," Enloe said suddenly, turning as he buttoned his shirt, "I want to ask you something—rather confidentially."

Rennert's face was impassive as his eyes followed the movements of Enloe's fingers. They were long, flexible fingers and looked strong.

"A certain member of this party," Enloe continued, "is not what he pretends to be."

He turned to select a tie from the side of the dresser. The room was suddenly very still.

"Is that so?" Rennert's voice was expressionless.

"Yes. I'm not going to mention any names, because I haven't any proof, but," his long fingers yanked savagely at the dark red tie, "this man is a damned skunk and before this trip is over I'm going to wring his neck." He pulled down the collar of his shirt and picked up a comb and brush. "I wanted to ask you, Rennert, if you knew who I mean."

Rennert watched Enloe comb and brush his hair. It was light brown hair, wiry, the color of the sands along the Rio Grande. It was cut short, but at the back, where the light from the chandelier fell upon it, was a thin line of gray, matching the line over the temples.

"I think," he said, "that I know who you mean."

"I expect you do." Enloe shot Rennert a quick glance as he walked toward the closet. "Do you think I'm right?"

His voice came slightly muffled from the close little room.

"Yes," Rennert said, "I think you are right."

"Do you *know?*"

Enloe was emerging from the closet. His hands were hidden behind a dark blue coat which he was inspecting carefully.

Rennert did not reply for a moment. He was watching Enloe as the latter walked slowly toward him. In the middle of the room he paused and brushed the collar and the lapels of the coat with a broad red hand.

"I know," Rennert said,

Enloe looked up quickly and regarded Rennert with narrowed eyes. When he pulled his eyelids down like that, Rennert thought, they looked oddly like little pig eyes.

"Good," he said slowly, the corners of his lips drawn slightly downward, "I'll remember that."

With a hasty movement he pulled on his vest and coat and buttoned them. He cast a glance downward at the sharp straight line of the crease in his trousers and at the polished surface of his shoes.

"Ready to go?" he asked.

"Yes."

Rennert got up and preceded Enloe out the door.

The corridor was quiet and the solitary electric bulb gave the dark walls a vault-like effect. The thick nap of the mulberry-colored carpet muffled the sound of their footsteps. Enloe took a handkerchief from his pocket and blew his nose. The walls cast the sound back and forth.

"I must finish my packing tonight," Rennert said as they stood before the elevator shaft. "I have a package to tie up and meant to buy some rope today, but forgot it."

Enloe pressed the button with a big square thumb. "Brody has some rope in the room," he said, "you can use it."

"He won't need it?"

"No, I don't suppose so—not after tonight." The huge cables in the shaft writhed and groaned like tortured serpents as the elevator slowly ascended. "Did Brody bring his lariat with him?" Rennert smiled, his eyes on the cables.

"No," Enloe laughed, "Brody doesn't use this rope as a lariat."

"I can't picture him using a rope for any other purpose."

The elevator came to a stop before them and the iron grille door slid open.

"You'd be surprised," Enloe said as he stepped in beside Rennert, "just what Brody does use this rope for."

16
"LET'S PLAY—"

THEY FOUND MOST of the members of the party already assembled in the little dining-room off the mezzanine floor which Dr. Lipscomb had reserved for his farewell dinner.

There was an air of animation about the room and a buzz of conversation greeted their ears. Everyone seemed in unusually good spirits, as usually happens when people who have seen much of one another for some time see the end of their association approaching.

Dr. Lipscomb, circulating about the room, his hair sleeked close to his head and a beam of delight on his face, found that his little jokes and geniality met with instant, unqualified response. Even the delay of Miss Tredkin and Brody failed to disturb his conviviality. He gave the suggestion of a wink to Enloe as he shook his hand, with the remark: "Your roommate seems to have found another attraction, Colonel."

At last the two belated ones made their appearance and they moved toward the long table in the center of the room.

The spirit of the fiesta had been carried out in the decorations. In the center of the table a realistic-looking skeleton of cardboard was perched upon a revolving pedestal, presenting to each of the guests in turn a gruesome, vacant face. In tall vases of Puebla pottery stood masses of orange-yellow *cempoalxochitl*, the Aztec death-flower, diffusing a sweetly pungent odor. The place cards were miniature skulls and crossbones.

They found their places, sat down and a waiter switched off the overhead lights, plunging the room into semidarkness. Over the table a row of tall candies masked behind grinning tissue-paper skulls threw an eerie light.

"Ooh!" Miss McCool's voice from across the table drew out the syllables, "Isn't this scary?"

"Dr. Lipscomb," Mrs. Willis said impressively, "I think you are to be congratulated upon your appointments. They are so original. They are—" She paused.

"Unique," her husband suggested.

"Yes, unique. I have never seen anything like them. Why, I feel almost afraid."

Rennert looked about him.

Dr. Lipscomb sat at the head of the table. A little ray of light fell full upon his face, combining with his set smile to give his countenance a curiously moonlike appearance. On either side of him were Mrs. Willis and Miss Tredkin. At the opposite end were Professor Bymaster, Tancel and Miss McCool. Rennert found himself between Mr. Willis, on his left, and Mrs. Earp, on his right. Beyond Mrs. Earp sat her husband and across the table were Brody, Argudin, Miss Dean and Enloe.

Conversation, general at first, soon found the same fate as commodities the world over and became a monopoly. Mrs. Willis, from her vantage point at the head of the table, soon drew Dr. Lipscomb, Miss Tredkin and Brody into the ambit of her reminiscences, which concerned mostly experiences with her husband's relations, who seemed to have colonized the Middle West in a rather thorough fashion. A second (or was it a third?) cousin of his lived in Wichita, two blocks from Miss Tredkin's home. This remarkable coincidence swept Miss Tredkin into the limelight for a few minutes, but the subject of Mr. Willis' cousin was soon exhausted and she retired into the background again.

At the other end of the table Miss McCool and Miss Dean kept the attention of the men about them with a running stream of jokes and commentaries upon the tour.

Argudin, equidistant between these two groups, seemed to belong to neither of them. He ate slowly, his attention concentrated upon his food. At the other end Professor Bymaster sat with folded arms, staring morosely into the vase of yellow flowers in front of him. He had, he informed Mrs. Earp, taken cold the day before and gave evidence of the fact by frequent sneezing.

"He looks," Mrs. Earp confided to Rennert in a rather loud whisper, "just like a mad little brown owl."

Rennert laughed.

He felt his companion's eyes studying his face. "That's the first time I ever heard you laugh like that, Mr. Rennert. I thought you were always serious."

"Not always, Mrs. Earp."

"I wish Ed would be more serious sometimes. I like serious men. Maybe he will when he realizes he's an old married man."

"How long have you folks been married, Mrs. Earp?"

"Let's see," her black, sticky-looking eyelashes closed over her eyes, "a week and a day. We were married the twenty-fifth and joined this party the next day. I think Mexico is a perfectly gorgeous place to come for a honeymoon." She was leaning a little closer to him and he caught the heady odor of strong perfume. "Didn't you just love Xochimilco?"

The waiter set coffee before them.

"Yes," Rennert agreed, "I did."

Mrs. Earp sipped the coffee and set it down with a little grimace of distaste.

"I don't like this Mexican coffee. It's so strong."

Rennert sensed a sudden lull in the conversation at his right. He saw Mrs. Willis lean over toward her husband and whisper something in his ear.

Mr. Willis arose and tapped with his spoon against a glass.

"Ladies and gentlemen," he began.

Miss McCool clapped her hands and cried "Hurrah!"

This seemed to disconcert Mr. Willis, for he stood for a moment and cleared his throat before continuing. Mrs. Willis glared at Miss McCool.

"Now that our pleasant association with one another is drawing to a close," the speaker's voice was too loud, "I am sure that we all feel a great deal of regret. For my part, I can say that I have enjoyed very much my friendship with you people and I hope that at some future time we can be together again. I know that you will all agree with me that a great deal of our pleasure has been due to the untiring efforts of Dr. Lipscomb to make our stay in Mexico a pleasant one. I suggest a toast to Dr. Lipscomb."

They drank and the conductor responded with a few stereotyped remarks. One knew that he had made them before and that he hoped to make them again.

A moment of silence followed the applause which his words drew. Someone began to push his chair back.

"Say," Miss McCool was on her feet, tapping upon her glass, "I don't think this party ought to break up so soon. It's an hour before the dance starts and we've all got time to put our costumes on. Why don't we play some kind of game?"

Applause, led by Miss Dean and Tancel, greeted the proposal.

"I know what let's do," Miss Dean spoke up; "it's just the thing for a spooky night like this. Let's play murder party!"

"Fine!" Miss McCool jerked her head back and forth in approbation. "What about it, Dr. Lipscomb? O.K. with you?"

Dr. Lipscomb, a startled look on his face, glanced around him. "Why, yes, of course, if the others wish."

"I think," Mrs. Willis was decisive, "that we are all rather tired and would prefer to go to our rooms."

"Aw, Mrs. Willis," Miss McCool protested, "don't break up the party. Let's play it. It's lots of fun."

"Well," Mrs. Willis glanced at her husband, "we might stay a few minutes and watch you."

"How do you play this game?" Brody asked.

Miss McCool grew voluble. "One of us pretends he's murdered and another one is the detective and tries to find out who killed him. You know—clews and alibis and all that."

"Say," Miss Dean was on her feet, "I have an even better idea. We don't need to pretend that there's been a murder. We already have a murder—a real one."

"What?" Dr. Lipscomb stared at her.

"Yes. You remember we spent one night at the Patio Hotel in San Antonio. Well," her words had been tumbling over one another and she paused for an instant, "the night we stayed there a man was murdered."

"Oh!" Rennert heard a little cry from Mrs. Earp and saw her husband put a steadying hand upon her shoulder.

"Let's pretend," Miss Dean went on, "that one of us murdered him. One of us will be the detective and try to find out which one of us is the most likely to have done it. Everybody will have alibis, of course, and the detective will try to break them, like they do in books."

"Great!" Miss McCool was vibrating with enthusiasm, "now who'll be the detective?" She looked about her.

"Dr. Lipscomb," Tancel suggested.

"No," she shook her head. "It ought to be somebody who wasn't in the hotel that night. Now, who wasn't there?"

"Brody wasn't," Colonel Enloe said.

"Nor Mr. Rennert," Argudin said softly from across the table. His black eyes were fixed on Rennert's face and a smile hovered about his lips.

"Mr. Rennert, he's the man!" Miss McCool exclaimed. "He didn't join us until we were already down here, so he won't know anything about what we all did that night except what he finds out by questioning us. Mr. Rennert, you're elected!"

"And listen," from Miss Dean, "everybody must take this seriously and tell the truth—except, of course, the murderer. He'll try to alibi out of it and Mr. Rennert will catch him."

"How will we decide which one of us did the murder?" Brody asked.

Miss McCool thought a moment. "Somebody give me a piece of paper," she demanded.

Tancel drew out an envelope and handed it to her.

"I'll tear this up into thirteen pieces," she said, "and I'll put a cross mark on one piece. Whoever draws that will be the murderer." Her fingers were at work upon the envelope.

"But tell us," Colonel Enloe said, "something about the circumstances of this murder that we're supposed to be covering up."

"Gertie can tell you all about it," Miss McCool said, without looking up; "she read all about it in the paper."

Everyone looked at Miss Dean.

"This man," she said slowly, "nobody seems to know who he was, was in a room on the fourth floor. We were all on the sixth floor, you remember. He was strangled with a pair of black silk stockings. It happened between eleven-thirty and midnight, the doctor said."

"And everybody's got to tell what he was doing at that time," Miss McCool was busy distributing the slips of paper. "Now one of these has a cross on it. Whoever draws that is the murderer."

Rennert, watching each person selecting one of the white slips, was thinking quickly.

Miss McCool finished the distribution of the slips and sat down.

A silence settled upon the room, broken only by the faint sputtering of the candles behind the yellow tissue paper.

"All right, Mr. Rennert," Miss Dean said, "we are ready."

17
"MURDER PARTY"

RENNERT GOT TO HIS FEET and glanced around the table. Whoever had drawn the marked paper had given no indication.

"I ought to have a pipe, a broad-brimmed hat and a microscope to do this right," he said with a smile, "but I'll do my best." He grasped his chin between thumb and forefinger and continued to look about him. He frowned.

"A man was murdered in the Patio Hotel in San Antonio," he said, "between eleven-thirty and midnight of August 27th. All of you, except Mr. Brody, were, I understand, staying in that hotel that night."

He looked squarely at Brody.

"Where were you that night?" he demanded.

Brody's face broke into a grin.

"Be serious now," Miss Dean reminded him.

The grin subsided a little. "I arrived in San Antonio at six-thirty Saturday morning—the morning the party left. I joined them at the station."

"Then you were on the train the night before?"

"Yes."

"Did you know any of these people before you met them at the station in San Antonio?"

"No."

"Do you have any idea who committed this murder?"

"Nary an idea."

"Very well," Rennert pursed his lips, "I shall now take each one of you in turn. Dr. Lipscomb, you are first. Where were you on the night of August 27th, between eleven-thirty and midnight?"

Dr. Lipscomb was sitting very straight in his chair. "I was," he said, "in bed."

"When did you go to bed?"

"About eleven o'clock."

"Did you hear any noise during the night?"

"No, I went to sleep at once. I was rather tired."

"Do you know if any member of your party owned a pair of black silk stockings?"

There was a snicker of laughter, quickly suppressed, at this.

The conductor's face flushed a trifle. He smiled rather forcedly.

"No, I do not."

"Very well, Dr. Lipscomb. Thank you."

Rennert turned suddenly upon Miss Tredkin. "Miss Tredkin," he pointed an accusing finger at her, "did you murder a man on the night of August 7th?"

She gasped. "Why, Mr. Rennert, of course not."

"Where were you on that night between eleven-thirty and midnight?"

"I was in bed." Her voice was low.

"In bed?" Rennert continued to look at her. "At what time did you go to bed?"

"Early, about nine-thirty. I always go to bed early."

"Miss Tredkin, do you or have you ever owned a pair of black silk stockings?"

Again she gasped and her face became suddenly scarlet. There was another snicker from the end of the table. From Tancel, Rennert thought.

"I have one pair," she said, her eyes fixed on her plate.

"What size?"

A pause. "9½."

"Do you still have them?"

"Yes, they are in my bag now."

"Did you have another pair when you started on this trip?"

"No, the rest were woolen. Dr. Lipscomb wrote me that it was cold down here, so I brought woolen ones."

"Very well, Miss Tredkin. Thank you."

She relaxed in her chair and glanced sideways at Brody, in whose eyes Rennert detected a twinkle of amusement.

"And now," Rennert said, "we come to Mr. Argudin."

Argudin sat with his chair tilted back from the table, his hands crossed upon his lap. He regarded Rennert steadily and his smile broadened.

"Where were you, Mr. Argudin, on the night of August 27th, between eleven-thirty and midnight?"

"I have an excellent alibi. I played bridge in the cardroom off the lobby from nine o'clock until one. I played with Miss McCool, Miss Dean and Mr. Tancel."

"You didn't leave the room during that time?"

Rennert saw Miss Dean's mouth open and as quickly close again. He turned to her.

"Is that right, Miss Dean? Did you play cards with Mr. Argudin from nine o'clock until one?"

"Yes, I did."

"Did any of you leave the room?"

"Yes."

"Mr. Argudin."

"At what time did he leave?"

"I don't remember for sure. It must have been about midnight, though. He said he wanted to get some cigarettes."

"How long was he gone?"

"About a quarter of an hour."

Rennert turned to Argudin. "Is that right?"

Argudin's face had not changed. "Yes," he said, "I had forgotten. I did go out to the drug store on the corner and buy some cigarettes. I was gone perhaps fifteen minutes." A little of the silky quality crept into his voice. "It was, I believe, about a quarter until twelve, or thereabouts, as Miss Dean has been kind enough to remind me."

"Did you go upstairs during that time?"

"No, I did not."

"Did you see any of these people in or about the hotel when you went out?"

"Yes. I saw Colonel Enloe enter the elevator when I came back."

"That would be about midnight?"

"Yes, that would be about midnight."

Rennert turned to Enloe. "Is this true, Colonel?"

Enloe nodded. "Yes," he said brusquely, "that's right, I got back to the hotel about midnight. I had spent the evening with some friends of mine, officers out at Post Field."

"Did you go at once to your room?"

"Yes."

"Did you stop at the fourth floor? Room 417, for instance?"

"Room 417?" Enloe's eyes met his. "Is that the room where the murder was committed?"

"Yes" (Rennert cursed himself inwardly for the slip), "we'll call it 417."

"No, I did not stop at the fourth floor."

"Did you see any of these people on the sixth floor when you went to your room?"

"Yes, I saw one of them."

"Who?"

Enloe was fingering the end of his mustache. "Really," he said, smiling, "I dislike to mention it—but I saw Professor Bymaster."

Rennert involuntarily let his eyes follow the others' to where Bymaster sat at the end of the fable. His mouth had fallen open and his round eyes behind the tortoise-shell spectacles gave him a more owlish expression than ever.

Rennert turned back to Enloe.

"Where was Dr. Bymaster?"

"He was coming in the door at the end of the hall, the one that opens onto the fire escape, I believe."

"Did he see you?"

"Yes, he spoke and went on to his room."

Rennert turned slowly to Bymaster.

"Is this true, Dr. Bymaster?"

For a moment the little man seemed unable to speak as his Adam's apple performed gymnastics. His thin hands were white against the white tablecloth; and he raised and lowered his fingers in a way that recalled the movement of a spider's legs. There were little tufts of brown hair below the knuckles.

"Yes," he managed, "it is true. I went to bed early, but I could not sleep. The room seemed so warm and close. I arose and walked down the hall to the rear door to get some fresh air."

"Did you go out on the fire escape?"

"Yes, I stepped out there for a few minutes."

"How long was it, Dr. Bymaster, between the time you left your room and the time you returned to it?"

"Not more than ten minutes." (The fingers were rising and falling with monotonous regularity.)

"Do you know the time?"

"I looked at my watch when I got back. It was ten minutes until twelve."

"Did you, during this time, hear any noise or see anyone, except Colonel Enloe on the sixth floor?"

Rennert considered for a moment. (That fire escape had been freshly painted. In that case there should still be traces of the paint. . . . He decided to let that wait for the present.)

"That will be all, Professor Bymaster."

He turned to Earp.

"And now it's your turn, Mr. Earp. The usual question, where were you on the night of August 7th, between eleven-thirty and midnight?"

Earp carefully flicked the ash from his cigarette into his coffee cup.

"In bed," he said; "we went to bed about ten-thirty, I think it was. We didn't hear any noise or see anybody until morning."

Rennert looked down at Mrs. Earp.

"I suppose you will vouch for that, Mrs. Earp?"

Her red lips parted in what she evidently meant for a smile.

"Yes, Mr. Rennert." He noticed that the fingers of her right hand were tight about the stem of a glass.

"Mrs. Earp, do you or did you when you started on this tour own a pair of black silk hose?"

"No."

"Do you know if any person in this party owned such a pair?"

She looked fixedly at the yellow flowers in front of her. "No, I don't know."

"Very well, then. And now," Rennert cleared his throat, "we come to you, Mr. Willis."

The jeweler sat forward in his chair.

"I can tell you what you want to know in a few words, Rennert. Mrs. Willis and I retired about ten-thirty or a little before. We were exhausted by our trip. We know nothing about all this."

"Mrs. Willis," Rennert looked at her intently, "did you own or do you now own a pair of black silk stockings?"

He continued to look at her as the color drained from her face, leaving it cold hard enamel. Her eyes sought her husband's.

"Did you?" he repeated.

Mr. Willis pushed back his chair and got to his feet. He turned to Dr. Lipscomb.

"I understood," he said, "that this was to be a game. It seems to be developing into a regular police interrogation. It may be amusing to some of these people, but it is not to my wife and myself. We have had enough of it and beg you to excuse us."

Dr. Lipscomb, too, arose.

"I think that Mr. Willis is right. It is getting late and I suggest that we close our little party. Some of you will doubtless want to dress for the ball," he glanced at his watch, "which will begin in half an hour. Now," he was wearing again his genial smile, "who was the murderer?"

There was a sizzling sound as the wax from one of the candles came into contact with the tissue paper about its base.

No one spoke.

Dr. Lipscomb looked from face to face.

"Who," he repeated, smiling more broadly, "was the murderer? The game is over now and it's time to confess. Who drew the paper with the cross mark?"

Rennert, still standing behind his chair, gazed up and down the table.

Dr. Lipscomb, Miss Tredkin, Brody, Argudin, Miss Dean, Enloe, Miss McCool, Tancel, Bymaster, the Earps and the Willises. Each person was doing the same.

"Why, that's funny," Miss McCool said, "I'm sure I marked one piece of paper. Maybe—"

Her head for once ceased its restless movements and she sat very still, her eyes on Rennert's.

"Oh, well," Dr. Lipscomb laughed, "it doesn't matter. I think that we all enjoyed the game."

Above the noise of chairs being pushed back and the renewed buzz of conversation, Miss McCool's voice was not too low to carry to Rennert's ears.

"Maybe—it wasn't a game."

18
DARKNESS

Si Adelita se fuera con otro
La seguiría la huella sin cesar—

SOMEWHERE, under one of those flat roofs that lay like a dark motionless sea outside the window, a phonograph sent through the still night air a reedy voice that sang, to the faint rhythmic accompaniment of a guitar, the soldier ballad of the deserts and the bleak sierras.

Rennert, as he undressed, found himself softly whistling the refrain. The inchoate yearnings of a race expressing itself—as always—in melancholy, even when it is happy. Chateaubriand would have understood these people. An incomplete instrument, the human heart, a lyre with missing cords. . . .

His telephone rang very softly.

Someone, the mechanical voice of the operator informed him, wished to speak to Mr. Rennert (the *r*'s trilled against his ear) on the Mexican system phone. Would he do the favor of going to the booth in the hall, where his call would be transferred?

He hung up the receiver of the Ericksson telephone, with which the hotel rooms were equipped, put on a dressing gown and walked down the hall. From the ballroom downstairs, muffled by passage through the corridors, came the faint echoes of the orchestra playing "If I Had a Talking Picture of You."

As he reached the little booth by the elevator the music stopped. There was the faint sound of applause. He closed the glass door behind him, took down the receiver.

112

"Hello."

There was no answer.

He spoke again, more sharply this time. He was vaguely aware of figures passing down the hall outside.

A sharp little click and the operator's voice, faint annoyance in the tone, came to him. Would Mr. Rennert pardon? The person who had been calling had left the line. If this person called again, she would ring the telephone in his room. Was it a man or a woman who had called? It was a woman.

Rennert slammed the door of the booth and walked down the hall. A masked figure, wearing the white plumes and the black cape of a traditional Don Juan, glanced at him as he passed. Probably wondering, Rennert said to himself, what I'm supposed to represent—a burgher roused from peaceful slumber by midnight revelry or a ghost in the trappings of the tomb on his way to a tryst.

Where could that call have been from? Who could be wanting to talk to him at this hour of the night?

Upon the threshold of his room he stopped. He had the queer feeling that there was a faint, sweetly pungent odor about the room. The draft between the open door and the window carried it away, however, still unrecognized.

He closed the door, tossed his dressing gown over a chair and switched off the light. He got into bed.

He lay for a time, hands clasped behind his head, and stared out the dark frame of the window at the stars.

> *Y si acaso yo muero en la lucha*
> *O en la sierra mi cuerpo ha de quedar—*

The reedy tenor had begun again. Softened by the distance, his plaint floated through the window. The underlying melody kept running through Rennert's head, disturbing, yet oddly in tune with his thoughts.

Like the undercurrent which he had sensed beneath the events of that day and of that night, giving warning of its presence by occasional ripples and eddies that broke the even stillness of the stream of existence of these oddly assorted people. Like the tension behind the smiling faces about that dinner table. . . .

(Was that telephone going to ring again?)

For an instant he had been on the point of crashing with one blow through this baffling, smiling quietness, of forcing each person who sat in that room to submit to a search, to find that damned, trifling piece of paper. Yet he had refrained, as he had refrained before from the same impulse.

Suppose he had found the paper? Someone would have smiled and explained plausibly enough that he—or she—had not noticed the tiny cross penciled thereon. Or that there had been a natural desire to avoid embarrassment.

That bit of paper began to assume proportions now. (Like that telephone call.)

Tomorrow—and the next day—when they were in the narrow confines of a train, speeding northward, there would be time. . . .

When he awoke, it was the stillness of the room that impressed his sharply awakened senses.

The room was very still.

Holding the rest of his body motionless, he raised his head slowly from the pillow and sent his eyes about the room.

Darkness lay about him like a shroud. Only the window was a faintly illuminated square, bounded by blackness.

A little breeze was coming in the window, tinkling the tiny crystals of the chandelier.

Slowly he reached for the automatic which lay upon the little table beside the bed. His fingers closed about the cold steel.

With a swift movement he sat up in bed and with his other hand pulled the cord of the bedlamp. A slight tick, but there was no answering illumination.

The darkness before him was as impenetrable as ever. A slight movement from the darker shape in front of the door that his eyes, accustomed now to the darkness, had made out. The figure moved forward a little, that was all.

Rennert raised his automatic, fired.

The figure (he saw now that it was tall and large, of uncertain, wavering outlines) moved forward noiselessly and unswervingly.

Rennert leveled his revolver again, took careful aim and fired twice in rapid succession.

The illuminated patch of the window was invisible now, blotted out by the black shape that was approaching the bed. It moved more swiftly now and the sweet, pungent odor enveloped him. Insanely his mind associated it with old, forgotten things. He sickened as he identified it.

Without lowering his arm Rennert fired again, then struck savagely with the barrel as he felt dry fingers at his throat.

PART THREE
MEXICO CITY–LAREDO

Mexico City	Lv.	8:10 A.M.
Queretaro	Ar.	2:12 P.M.
Queretaro	Lv.	2:32 P.M.
San Luis Potosí	Ar.	8:35 P.M.
San Luis Potosí	Lv.	8:55 P.M.
Monterrey	Ar.	8:00 A.M.
Monterrey	Lv.	8:25 A.M.
Nuevo Laredo	Ar.	2:00 P.M.

19
MRS. RANKIN IS LATE

COLONIA STATION, MEXICO CITY, 8:10 A.M.
TO LAREDO, 1291 KILOMETERS

"*A BORDO.*"

The conductor's warning call was relayed down the station platform to where Dr. Lipscomb stood at the steps of the last Pullman.

Dr. Lipscomb was in a state of agitation. He thrust his watch into his pocket for the last time and fell to pinching the end of his mustache between thumb and forefinger. He took a few hasty steps toward the huge iron gate which separated him from the station, then turned back.

Far ahead the engine was emitting puffs and janglings.

He set one polished shoe on the lowest step, grasped the bars at the side and cast a last despairing glance toward the iron gate.

With a hasty exclamation he put his foot back upon the platform, released the bars and signaled desperately in the general direction of the front of the train.

The iron gate opened and clanged shut again behind Mrs. Rankin.

She moved with unhurried steps toward the train, glancing leisurely about her; once (Dr. Lipscomb could have jumped up and down in his impatience) she paused in a bit of sunlight and looked at the sky.

"Mrs. Rankin," the conductor's voice was a sigh of relief, "I thought you were going to miss the train."

119

She threw her head backward a little and laughed lightly.

"Oh, Dr. Lipscomb, I am so sorry, but you see I have learned my lesson from Mexico. Time isn't so important to me as it used to be."

He took from her hand the little black bag and helped her up the steps.

"Your luggage is all in the car," he said; "what would you have done if you had missed the train?"

She turned her head to smile at him.

"There is another train always and one has a lifetime to wait."

They entered the Pullman and he put the bag on the seat opposite hers. Then he took off his hat and ran a hand over his forehead.

"Everybody's here," he said, his eyes roving over the car. "We are ready to start."

The Pullman was a scene of confusion. On one side of them Earp, a black beret pulled jauntily over his forehead, was on his knees trying to shove a hat box under the seat. On the other side Mrs. Willis was conducting a frantic search for a lost package. It contained, she informed Dr. Lipscomb, some pottery which she had bought at Puebla. She had told Mr. Willis to put it in one of the bags, but it wasn't there now. Dr. Lipscomb stood by, looking sympathetic, while the harassed Mr. Willis ransacked their luggage.

Tancel and Colonel Enloe were aiding Miss McCool and Miss Dean in the adjustment of a number of packages, all marked "Fragile." Brody was standing while Miss Tredkin handed him various articles to put in the rack above their heads. Professor Bymaster was engaged in arranging papers in his brief case.

In the rear seat upon their right, aloof from the turmoil, sat Argudin, gazing intently out the window. His face was lifelessly pale, an effect heightened by the strip of white plaster which covered the right side of his chin.

Mrs. Rankin removed her hat and placed it on the seat opposite. Her white fingers smoothed her hair as she stood glancing up and down the car.

"And where," she asked as Dr. Lipscomb turned toward the front of the car (Mrs. Willis had just remembered that she had at the last moment put the missing package in the trunk) "is Mr. Rennert?"

Dr. Lipscomb drew from his pocket a sheaf of railway tickets and began to run through them hastily.

"Mr. Rennert," he said, "is not going back with us."

"Not going back?" her fingers were suddenly still. "Why, he told me last night that he was."

"He must have changed his mind. He has decided to remain in Mexico City."

20
"ONE OF YOU—"

"Dr. Lipscomb!"

The conductor of the Inter-America Tours, Inc., looked up quickly at the speaker, a little frown of annoyance upon his face. (He had been engaged, with the aid of a hand mirror and a moistened forefinger, in smoothing down his eyebrows, which had a distressing habit of standing out at right angles to his head. This operation he always preferred to perform in privacy.)

"Yes, Colonel Enloe?" (He slipped the mirror into his pocket, hoping that the colonel hadn't noticed it. By no flight of the imagination could one picture him smoothing down his eyebrows.)

"I just started to go up in the next car. At the door I was stopped by a soldier or a policeman or some sort of official. What does it mean?"

Dr. Lipscomb's mouth fell open. "A policeman?" he echoed.

"I suppose he's a policeman or a soldier; he is wearing a uniform—and a revolver. He jabbered at me in Spanish, but I couldn't tell what he said."

Dr. Lipscomb got to his feet.

"I can't imagine," he said, "what the trouble is. I'll see."

He felt a touch upon his shoulder and turned.

A small thin man in the nondescript uniform of the Mexican army stood at his elbow.

"Dr. Lipscomb?" he inquired politely.

"Yes, I am Dr. Lipscomb. What is it?"

"Will you be kind enough to come with me into the next car?"

"What for?" The brusqueness of his voice failed to be convincing.

The man shrugged expressively and gestured with one hand in the direction of the car ahead.

Dr. Lipscomb preceded him down the aisle and into the next car. He was conscious of a suppressed air of excitement and of the eyes of the entire party centered upon him. Try as he might, he could not prevent his face from going red.

At the door he stopped and stared at the man who sat in the first seat, facing him.

"Come in, Dr. Lipscomb," Rennert said, "and sit down."

Rennert's face was unnaturally pale and his brown eyes were shot through with little red veins. His shirt was open at the throat, revealing a white cloth against the skin.

"Why, Mr. Rennert," Lipscomb said as he sat on the edge of the seat opposite, "I thought that you had decided to stay in Mexico City."

Rennert's face had a metallic fixity.

"Why did you think that?"

"Why, your note."

"My note?"

"Yes, I found under my door this morning a note from you, saying that you had discovered that you were mistaken about the man you were looking for being among my guests and that you had decided to remain in Mexico City."

Rennert continued to look at him.

"Do you have that note with you?"

Dr. Lipscomb shook his head. "I don't think so," he said. He drew several letters from his pockets and glanced through them hastily. "No, I do not have it. I believe I tossed it in the wastebasket."

"Was the note written by hand?"

"No, it was typewritten."

"And the signature?"

"Written with a pen." Lipscomb's face paled to a perceptible degree. "Do you mean, Mr. Rennert, that you did not write that note?"

"No, I did not write that note."

The other's hands, resting upon his knees, tightened.

"I am sorry," he said, "but it was not my fault. I had never seen your signature. I had no cause to suspect that the note was forged."

Rennert was silent for a moment.

"Were you in your room last night?" he asked.

"Yes, after about eleven o'clock. After dinner I went to the ballroom and remained for a while, watching the dancing. Then I went to my room and retired."

"Were all the members of your party at the ball?"

"I believe that most of them paused for a few moments after dinner to look at the costumes, but only a few of them stayed for the evening."

"Which ones stayed?"

"I do not know."

"You do not know?"

"No, you see it was a masquerade ball and all the dancers wore costumes and masks. I really do not know which guests of mine were on the floor."

Rennert became thoughtful.

"Do you know," he asked, "what costumes any of your party intended to wear?"

"No, I do not."

"Did you hear any disturbance during the night, Dr. Lipscomb?"

"I was awakened by some kind of a noise upstairs, I believe, but I paid no attention to it. I supposed it as just a part of the celebration."

The color had begun to creep back into his cheeks.

"What happened during the night, Mr. Rennert?"

"About three o'clock someone entered my room and attempted to strangle me, very nearly succeeded. When the elevator boy and some of the guests in the adjoining rooms got to me, a rope had been knotted about my neck and knotted again to the bedpost. It was some time, however, before they located the sound of the shots, since the lights on my floor had been turned off at the switch in the hall. In the meantime my—guest had escaped."

The color had drained from Lipscomb's cheeks again. "The shots!" he asked. "You fired at the man?"

"Yes."

"Did you hit him?"

Rennert's gaze was impersonal. "No," he said, "I did not hit him."

"Your aim must be very poor," Dr. Lipscomb's smile was weak.

Rennert did not smile. "On the contrary," he said, "my aim is, I believe, very good."

The conductor's hands slowly clasped and unclasped about his knees.

"You are sure, then, that one of my guests attacked you last night?"

"Yes. This morning there would doubtless have been a 'Do Not Disturb' sign on my door and my body would not have been found until this train was well on its way to the border."

"But didn't you have your door locked?"

"Yes, the doors of the hotel have automatic locks, you remember. After I had undressed I was called to the telephone in the hall. While I was there someone entered my room and took the key. I did not miss it when I returned."

Rennert arose.

"Your party are all in the Pullman back there, I understand."

"Yes, they are all there."

"Dr. Lipscomb, you and every member of your party are, practically speaking, under arrest."

"Arrest!"

Dr. Lipscomb had started to arise, but now sank back on his seat.

"Yes. No one will be allowed to leave that car, except to go to the diner, until we cross the border tomorrow. At that time I shall deliver the murderer over to the Texas authorities."

Dr. Lipscomb's Adam's apple started to work uncertainly.

"This is terrible, Rennert," he managed at last. "Terrible. It will ruin me."

"I am sorry, but it cannot be avoided. If you will accompany me back into the other car, I shall question some of your guests."

Lipscomb started to speak, then shut his lips tightly. He got to his feet and moved dazedly toward the rear.

Rennert hurriedly wrote a few lines on a piece of paper and handed it to the uniformed man who had remained impassively at his side during his interview with Dr. Lipscomb.

"See that this telegram is sent off at the next station," he said.

The man nodded.

Rennert followed Dr. Lipscomb into the rear Pullman. As he made his way through the passage he was aware of an excited buzz of conversation. At the doorway he paused.

The car was suddenly silent.

He stood for a moment, looking over the faces turned toward him. Most of the party were grouped about the Willises in the center of the car.

"If you will all sit down," he said quietly, "I have something to say to you."

He watched them as they moved quickly to seats. His eyes rested for an instant on Mrs. Rankin, her pearl-like face unchanged as her fingers paused briefly in their mechanical manipulation of her knitting needles; they moved on to the Willises, sitting upright in one seat, while across the aisle Mrs. Earp, her lips two arcs of red against a face of white enamel, clutched the sleeve of her husband's coat; they passed from Miss Dean and Miss McCool, huddled closely together, to Tancel, his face turned backward to stare at Rennert; they took in the frowns with which Enloe and Brody greeted his appearance, Miss Tredkin's quivering lips and Bymaster's owlish stare; last of all, they paused at the rear, where Argudin sat, feet propped up on the seat opposite. Argudin's white teeth flashed in a smile as his eyes met Rennert's, a smile rendered grotesque by the plaster which pulled down the corner of his mouth.

Rennert looked for some time at this strip of plaster and, when he spoke, he pitched his voice to carry exactly to Argudin's small, fragile-looking ears. He said:

"I must introduce myself to you—again. I am an agent of the United States Treasury Department—"

"Oh!" Mrs. Willis' cry was quickly muffled behind a handkerchief, over the top of which her eyes, round with fear, stared at him.

"My original mission is not pertinent to this inquiry. It has become negligible beside a much more important matter. One of our men was strangled in the Patio Hotel in San Antonio on the night you stayed there. Our little game last night was, you see, serious after all. Because one of you murdered him."

At the rear there was the sound of sudden whimpering. Miss Tredkin's face was buried on Brody's shoulder as with a big red paw he patted her head.

Willis was on his feet.

"Rennert," his voice was shrill with anger, "this is an outrage! You have no right to carry on an inquisition like this, to frighten these women. If you think that somebody in this car murdered that man, arrest him and don't draw us into it."

"Unfortunately, Mr. Willis," Rennert's voice hardened, "several of this party—including yourself—*are* drawn into this business. I am afraid that I must impress upon you your position. You are in Mexico at present; tomorrow you will be in the United States. Both governments want one person in this party—for different reasons. It is my intention that this case be brought to an end in the United States. However, the government of Mexico has put at my disposal soldiers with authority to arrest any person whom I may indicate. Which means, so to speak, that you are between the devil and the deep blue sea. Do you have anything more to say?"

Willis shook his head and sank onto his seat.

"Now," Rennert's eyes traveled slowly from face to face, "it becomes my duty to inquire into several things. This may involve bringing to light rather unpleasant personal details in the case of a few of you. There is one course which will save us all this trouble and unpleasantness. The person who strangled our man in San Antonio is in this car right now. I am now speaking to him—or her. Will you confess?"

"Her?" Miss Dean echoed. She was perched upon the arm of the seat, her eyes fixed eagerly upon Rennert's face. Alone of the group she seemed perfectly natural, as if she were enjoying the experience. "Do you think maybe it's a woman, Mr. Rennert?"

"I do not know, Miss Dean. It is possible."

"Oh," her head shot forward (like, the insanely inapropos thought flashed into his mind, a turtle's out of a shell) "so you don't know who it is?"

"No," he said gravely, "I do not know who it is."

He took out his watch, ran his thumb over the face of it.

"I am going," he said, "to give you—the murderer—three minutes to decide. Think it over."

He looked steadily at the watch.

Silence settled upon the car, broken only by the steady rhythmic hum of the rails beneath them. Below the lowered blind of the window beside Mrs. Rankin the sunlight entered in a long thin beam. It struck the bright steel knitting needles upon her lap and sent a wavering reflection against Rennert's left cheek.

"One minute," he said quietly.

At the rear of the car Miss Tredkin broke again into soft whimpering. Someone was breathing hoarsely. Rennert caught the sound of whispering.

"Two minutes," he said.

The whispering stopped abruptly, began again in a lower tone, until it fused with the hum of the rails. When Professor Bymaster sneezed suddenly, it seemed that a tremor ran through the car.

"Three minutes."

Rennert looked up as his hand replaced the watch in his pocket. His eyes traveled very slowly about the little group.

"The time is up. It would have been better if you had confessed."

"I want," Mr. Willis said wearily, "to make a statement."

21
EXPLANATIONS

Lechería, 8:49 a.m.
To Laredo, 1269 kilometers

WILLIS GOT SLOWLY to his feet and rested one hand upon the back of the seat.

"Will you please go into the drawing-room, Mr. Willis," Rennert said quietly.

Willis walked down the aisle, his shoulders stooped.

Rennert followed him. At the door he stopped and gave directions to the soldier who stood there. He turned and said:

"I am directing that you give this man any weapons which you may have. You will please open your luggage, so that he may search it. This applies to each and every one of you."

He turned his back on them, as a low murmur of protest arose, and went into the drawing-room.

Willis sat in a chair, his legs crossed. His lower lip was pressed tightly between his teeth and his face looked tight and drawn, immeasurably older.

Rennert sat down opposite him and regarded him for a moment.

"All right, Mr. Willis," he said, "I should like to hear what you have to say."

Willis released his lip and sighed wearily.

"It's about those damned stockings," he looked squarely into Rennert's eyes.

"Yes?"

"I feel sure I bought the pair that that man was strangled with."
He passed a hand over his forehead. "I should have said something
about it sooner, I know, I should have notified the San Antonio
police. But I didn't know anything about the murder until we got
to Mexico City, when I read about it in a newspaper. It was the
first vacation I had had in years and I didn't want to have it ruined
by anything like this. I talked it over with Mrs. Willis and we decided to say nothing until we were in San Antonio again on our
way back. We fully intended then, however, to go to the police with
the story.

"It is a little embarrassing for us, but I feel that I should tell
you everything. My wife is," he paused and studied intently the
nail of his right thumb, "rather trying sometimes."

He looked up and his gaze met Rennert's. "I don't suppose you
know what I mean, not being married."

Rennert's face took on a careful lack of expression.

"I have an idea," he said.

"Well, in the confusion of getting started, one of our bags was
left at home. I don't know whose fault it was—mine, probably. But
it contained a lot of her clothes. She was rather—ah, difficult about
it when she found it out. Kept referring to it, blaming it on me.
Among other things, the bag had all her stockings in it. She didn't
discover that, however, until we were in San Antonio and she went
to get dressed. I told her that I would go and buy her a pair."

He shifted his position in the chair and his eyes fell to the floor.

"I never paid any particular attention to the color of the stockings my wife wore. I don't think any man who has been married as
long as I have does. I went in the first store I came to and asked
for a pair of silk stockings. The girl at the counter asked me about
the size and color. I said the first thing that came in my mind—
black—and guessed at the size.

"When I got back to the room and Mrs. Willis saw the stockings she said that she wouldn't wear them, that no woman would
wear black stockings. I asked her why she hadn't told me what color
to get. She said that she thought I cared enough for her to notice
the color she wore. I said—" his eyes closed wearily, "but there's

no use in going into all that. I lost my temper, took the stockings and threw them out in the hall. That's the last I saw of them."

"What time was that, Mr. Willis?"

"About six o'clock," he opened his eyes and stared out the window behind Rennert. "That night this man was strangled with them. Someone must have picked them up in the hall."

"Yes," Rennert said absently, "someone picked them up. That will be all, Mr. Willis. I wish that you had told me this sooner."

The jeweler got to his feet and left the room.

After the door had closed, Rennert sat for a time, staring thoughtfully at the chair which the other man had occupied. Mechanically he took from his pocket a package of cigarettes, selected one and lit it. Not until it was quite gone did he get up and walk to the door. He beckoned to the soldier outside. The man handed him two revolvers (Enloe's Colt .45 and Earp's Smith & Wesson). Rennert examined them and handed them back to the soldier.

"Put them in one of my bags," he directed. "There was nothing else?"

"No, sir, there was nothing else."

Rennert followed him out and glanced over the occupants of the Pullman.

"Mr. Brody," he called, "will you come in here, please."

The big man got to his feet and lumbered down the aisle. In the drawing-room he eased himself into a chair and regarded Rennert uncertainly.

"Say, Rennert," he said abruptly, "why don't you be reasonable about this business? You think you've got a murderer cornered in this bunch. Maybe you're right, I don't know. But what's the use of scaring these women like this? Miss Tredkin, poor thing, has a weak heart and can't stand a sudden shock. Why don't you let those of us who aren't suspected go into another car or stop at San Luis Potosí or some place?"

"Because, Mr. Brody, suspicion falls on too many of you."

"Of us?" The blood rushed into Brody's face. "What do you mean?"

"Just that." Rennert's hand went to his pocket. He drew out a length of cotton rope and laid it across his knee. "Did you ever see this rope before, Brody?"

The other stared at it. The expression on his face was comical, almost, in its surprise.

"Why, yes, I had that rope or one just like it—at the hotel in Mexico City."

"And when did you last see this rope?"

Rennert's eyes were fixed on Brody's face as he let the soft strands run through his fingers. Brody shifted uneasily in his chair.

"Why, I don't remember exactly. Yesterday evening, I believe, before supper. If I remember right, I left it laying on a chair, or the foot of the bed, or some place. Why? What's it got to do with this business?"

"Last night," Rennert said quietly, "someone tried to strangle me with this rope."

22
THE ROPE

BRODY STARED, open-mouthed. Little dark red veins stood out against his pink cheeks.

"Well, I'll be damned!" he ejaculated. "What time last night?"

"About three o'clock this morning." Rennert continued to regard him steadily. "When did you leave your room last night, Brody?"

"About six. Miss Tredkin went with me to do some shopping. We got back to the hotel about seven and I put my bundles in my room, then we went to Doc Lipscomb's party. We went to a show afterwards and got back about eleven-thirty. I went to my room right away."

"Was Colonel Enloe there?"

"Yes. He was having a little party. There was a bunch of people there."

"Who?"

"Oh, let's see. Miss McCool and Miss Dean were there, and that Tancel fellow and the Earps. There were some strangers, too, I think. Everybody was drinking and having a good time and I didn't notice particular who was there."

"You didn't see the rope anywhere in the room when you went back?"

"No."

"And how long did they stay?"

"'Til about one o'clock, I think."

"Were any of them in costume?"

"The two girls were—some sort of green and white and red dresses, with spangles on 'em. Tancel had on a sheet and a mask. The Earps had on their ordinary clothes."

"Did you see anyone," Rennert leaned forward a little, "who wore a long black cape and a hat with plumes?"

Brody thought a moment, then shook his head. "No, I never saw anybody dressed like that—I'm sure."

"When did you go to bed, Brody?"

"Right after that bunch left."

"Did Enloe go to bed then, too?"

"No, he went out with the others. He'd run out of likker and Tancel said he had some in his room. So they went down there. They wanted me to go, too, but I was sleepy and wanted to hit the hay. Besides," he fingered a huge ring set with a brilliant red stone, "I've quit drinking."

"And when did Enloe get back to the room?"

"I don't know, I didn't hear him come in. He was there in the morning. I'm a pretty sound sleeper, you see."

"I see."

Rennert slowly coiled the rope about his hand and slipped it into his pocket. "I'd like to know, Brody," he said, "just what you used this rope for."

Confusion spread like a wave over Brody's face. "Aw, Rennert," he said awkwardly, "I'd rather not say."

"I think, Mr. Brody, that you had better."

Brody was silent for a moment.

"Well," he broke into a laugh, "I guess I might as well. You see, it's this way—I've been used all my life to a kinda hard life riding and living out in the open. Lately I've been doing nothing but sitting around the house getting fat, doing nothing but eat and sleep. I didn't realize it 'til I got down here, but I've been acting like I was an old worn-out plowhorse, fit for nothing but to be shot. But I'm only 58, Rennert—lots of time yet to really live and travel around and see things. I just now realize what all I've been miss-ing—"

Rennert's smile was pleasant. "And the rope?"

"I decided to get rid of some of this fat, so I cut down on the grub and began to take more exercise. I've been doing half an hour of it twice a day, jumping rope and setting-up exercises and all that. That's what I got the rope for. I've lost five pounds, too," he concluded proudly.

Rennert arose, still smiling.

"That'll be all now, Brody. Glad you cleared things up."

There was a sheepish grin on Brody's face as he got to his feet. At the door he paused.

"Say, Rennert," he said, "you won't tell anybody about what I said, will you? They'd think I was an old fool."

"No," Rennert laughed. "I won't tell anybody. And," he added, as Brody opened the door, "you might tell Colonel Enloe to step in here, if you don't mind."

The train had halted at a small station. Beyond the stone depot stretched a dusty street, blank whitewashed adobe walls rising on either side. The painted front of a *pulqueria* was a splash of color halfway up the short street. Further on were visible the flat thatched roofs of adobe huts and towering in the background the blue mountains.

Rennert sat idly regarding the scene until Colonel Enloe entered.

He was spruce and immaculate as ever in a dark gray suit with minute stripes of a lighter color running through it. His eyes, how-ever, looked heavy-lidded and slightly bloodshot as he sat in a chair and looked at Rennert questioningly.

With one finger he stroked listlessly at his mustache.

"See here, Rennert," he began brusquely, "I want to be of every assistance to you which I can, but I know nothing at all of this busi-ness. Your words a while ago came as a complete surprise to me. My first thought was that you had lost your mind. I couldn't con-ceive of anyone in this party committing a murder.

"The more I think of it, though, the more I believe that you may be right. I've had a little experience with some of your men

and they usually know what they're about. So, if I knew of anything that would be of assistance to you, I should at once inform
you. But," his fingers gave a final twitch to his mustache and came
down on the arm of the chair, "I know of nothing."

"I should like," Rennert said, "to know more of last night."

"Last night?"

"Yes. I understand that you had several guests in your room."

"Well, what of it?"

"Someone took from your room last night a piece of rope."

"Brody's jumping rope?"

"Yes. That person entered my room this morning about three
o'clock and attempted to strangle me with that rope."

Enloe's eyes narrowed slowly. "So, that's what it was," he said.
"I heard Brody just now saying that someone had tried to strangle
you last night, but I didn't wait to hear any of the details."

"When did you last see this piece of rope, Colonel?"

"It was lying over the foot of the bed when we came in the room
about ten o'clock. I remember seeing it then. That's the last I remember of it."

"Who were your guests last night, Colonel?"

"The Earps, those two schoolmarms from Texas, Tancel and two
or three people staying in the hotel whom I met down at the dance.
I don't remember their names."

"When did your party break up?"

"We left my room about one o'clock, I think. Supplies had run
out and Brody wanted to go to bed, I knew. We went down in
Tancel's room then. Frankly, I don't know what time it was when
we quit. I drank quite a bit and have just a hazy recollection of
getting to bed. It must have been almost morning—at least I feel
like it now." He evidenced this feeling with a yawn.

"Did anyone leave Tancel's room before you did?"

"Good lord, Rennert, I can't remember! Probably so. You know
how things get after a few drinks. Everybody running around and
cutting up. Anyone could have left the room and," he regarded
Rennert from under heavy lids, "could have gone down to your

room about three o'clock, if that's what you mean, could have come
back without being missed."

He suddenly laid both palms flat on the arms of the chair and
leaned forward.

"But I can tell you this, Rennert—you're on the wrong track if
you think any of that crowd did it. In the first place, I don't think
any of them has the makings of a strangler. In the second place,
they were all too drunk to even find your room. I imagine they all
had trouble enough finding their own—I know I did. In the third
place," his voice dropped slightly, "there's only one person in this
party whom I would ever suspect for a minute. I think you know
who I mean."

Rennert's eyes rested for a moment on Enloe's face.

"You mean, of course, Argudin."

"Yes. If any man in that car out there is the man you want, it's
him. He hasn't got the guts to murder a man with a gun, but it
would be just about his level to sneak into a man's room and
strangle him while he's asleep. I've had some experience with these
stranglers and I'd say that Argudin's the type. I'm not making any
accusation, you understand, because I haven't any proof. This is
just confidential, from one who has been in the United States service, to one who's in it now. And, say," his eyes were suddenly wide
open, staring at Rennert, "I've just remembered something.
Argudin was in my and Brody's room last night!"

Rennert's eyes narrowed slightly this time. He said nothing but
continued to regard the other thoughtfully.

"I don't know why I didn't think of it before," Enloe continued,
a little breathlessly; "my mind's not very clear this morning.
Argudin busted into our party about eleven or eleven-thirty. He
asked, of all things, if any of us wanted to play cards. That made
me see red at first but I told him that we would play. He said that
he'd go down and get some new cards. I told him that I would go
with him. He didn't want me to but I went anyway. Then he happened to remember that he had a new deck in his room and so
there wasn't any use buying another one." He paused. "We decided

not to play cards and Argudin didn't go back to the room with me." His fingers closed about the arms of the chair. "I believe, Rennert, that he's your man! He could have slipped that rope in his pocket without our seeing it."

Beneath them the rails hummed in drowsy monotone. The morning sun beat down upon the lowered blinds and entered between them and the sill to shine blindingly upon Colonel Enloe's polished brown shoes.

Rennert's silence seemed to make Enloe nervous. He shifted in his chair. "Want me any more?" he asked.

"No, Colonel, not at present," Rennert smiled pleasantly, "and many thanks for your help."

"That's all right, don't mention it."

He got to his feet and started toward the door.

"By the way," Rennert said, "I notice that Argudin has a plaster on his chin this morning."

Enloe grunted.

"Yes, he has—those cards were marked."

23
THE DORMOUSE AND THE MAD HATTER

TEOCALCO, 10:09 A.M.
TO LAREDO, 1207 KILOMETERS

"WELL?"

Earp settled himself in the chair and threw one long leg over the other. He had failed to shave that morning and the light stubble upon his long jaws and slightly protuberant chin combined with the black beret to lend a curious Byronic attractiveness to an ordinarily somewhat weak face. His clear slate-blue eyes regarded Rennert idly under partially drawn lids.

"You have probably heard about last night, Earp?"

"Yes, it's a general topic of conversation out there." A gesture of the head indicated the Pullman. "I suppose you want an alibi from me."

"Yes."

"Enloe told you about the party, I suppose?"

"Yes."

"Well, the wife and I were there—in Enloe's room at first and later in Tancel's. We left about two o'clock and went to bed. We'd both had too much to drink and didn't wake until morning. Didn't hear any disturbance during the night."

"Were you in costume last night, Earp?"

"No, we talked about dressing up, but decided it wouldn't be worth the trouble."

"I was wondering if you noticed anyone last night—a man about your height—wearing a long flowing cloak, a hat with plumes and a mask."

"No, I don't remember. We didn't stay at the dance very long. We— Say, wait a minute," he raised his eyelids and looked at Rennert intently. "Seems to me I do remember some fellow dressed like that. Long white plumes? A black mask?"

Rennert nodded.

"While we were down in Tancel's room a fellow came in dressed something like that, I think. I wouldn't say for sure, because he just stepped inside the door and said, 'Everybody having a good time?' or something like that, then went out again. I didn't see him again. That must have been just before we left."

Rennert stared at him thoughtfully.

"That's the first time anyone has mentioned this man being present."

Earp shrugged a shoulder.

"Most of them were too drunk to notice. It was a come and go affair, anyway. There were several people there—ones Enloe had picked up—that I'd never seen before. And this bird in the comic opera outfit didn't stay but a few seconds."

"I see." Rennert smiled pleasantly. "There's something else, Earp, I want to ask you about."

Earp held a cigarette poised before his lips. "Yes?" His eyes narrowed slightly.

"I notice that there is a tag missing from one of your pieces of luggage—one of those little red tags of the Inter-America Tours."

Earp slipped the cigarette into the corner of his mouth. "Well," his soft voice was almost a drawl, "what of it?"

Rennert's gaze was steady. "Just this, Earp. One of those tags was found under the body of the man who was strangled to death in San Antonio."

Except for a slightly increasing pressure of the lips against the cigarette not a muscle of Earp's face moved. One hand moved slowly to the pocket of his coat and brought out a lighter. He flipped it and applied the flame to the cigarette. He returned the lighter to his pocket and looked at Rennert, his eyes drawn into a little squint to escape a rising eddy of smoke.

"Not much to go on, is it, Rennert?" he asked quietly.

"It happens that only two pieces of luggage in this party do not have those tags—your suitcase and a trunk belonging to another member of the party."

"I see." Earp let his head fall backward and slowly blew a smoke ring toward the ceiling. "You'd better concentrate, then, on the other person, because that suitcase never did have a tag on it. I bought it in San Antonio the afternoon before we left."

"Dr. Lipscomb didn't give you a tag for it, then?" Earp was studying Rennert's face.

"No," he said.

Rennert returned the gaze. "Dr. Lipscomb says that he *did* give you a tag."

One of Earp's feet tapped gently against the floor, in time with the pulsating rhythm of the wheels. The set expression of his face did not alter as he said:

"Dr. Lipscomb is right; I had forgotten. He gave me a tag at the hotel in San Antonio."

"And what became of that tag, Earp?"

Earp's gaze strayed momentarily to the window behind Rennert. "I don't know," he said, "I must have lost it. I never thought about it again until now."

"You didn't attach it to your suitcase?"

"No, I'm sure I didn't."

"Your wife may remember what became of it?"

A lithe current of air carried another smoke ring toward the window as Earp said: "Possibly."

Rennert got to his feet.

"Suppose," he said, "that we ask Mrs. Earp about that tag."

Earp sat motionless, regarding Rennert fixedly. "See here," he said, "do you consider that tag important?"

"Yes," Rennert answered, "I do."

Earp took his cigarette from his mouth and carefully aimed it at a cuspidor.

"Well," he drawled, arising, "we'll hope Mrs. Earp remembers what became of it. I'd hate to go to the chair for a little thing like that."

Rennert smiled pleasantly as he held the door open.

"Smaller things than that," he said, "have sent men there."

As he entered the Pullman behind Earp, Rennert was conscious of a sudden lull in the conversation and of thirteen pairs of eyes centered upon him.

Mrs. Earp's eyes were round blue agates fixed on his face as she moved over in the seat. Her husband sank down beside her and gave the chubby hand which rested upon the green plush a reassuring pat.

Rennert returned Mrs. Rankin's smile and sat down opposite the Earps. His eyes lingered a moment on the flying steel needles across the aisle before he looked at Mrs. Earp.

"How are you this morning, Mrs. Earp?"

Her lips quivered slightly. "All right," she answered uncertainly.

Earp's fingers interlaced with hers.

"Mr. Rennert," he laughed, "wants to ask you a question, honey."

"Me?" she gasped.

The fingers of her left hand closed convulsively about the end of the long green scarf which hung beside the window.

"Yes, Mrs. Earp," Rennert indicated the suitcase which rested upon the seat at his side. "Do you happen to remember what became of the tag which Dr. Lipscomb gave Mr. Earp to put on this?"

"No," she shook her head slowly, "I don't remember."

"You see, honey," Earp's hand closed about hers and his voice grew gentle. "One of those tags was found under the body of that man who was strangled in San Antonio and Mr. Rennert, naturally, wants to find out who lost it. I told him that I didn't remember what became of the one that Dr. Lipscomb gave me in San Antonio, after I bought that new suitcase. You don't remember?"

"No," the color which had drained from her cheeks at Earp's first words began slowly to return. "I don't remember anything about the tag."

"And about last night, Mrs. Earp—do you remember seeing a tall man dressed in a black cloak, a hat with plumes and wearing a mask?"

"Oh, yes, Mr. Rennert, I remember a man dressed like that sticking his head in the door of Mr. Tancel's room while we were down there. I didn't know who he was, though, and he didn't stay. Just asked if everybody was having a good time and went out again."

"Mrs. Earp," Rennert asked quickly, "would you recognize his voice if you heard it again?"

For an instant a calculative look came into her blue eyes.

"I might," she said in a low voice.

"Had you heard it before?"

"I think that I had."

Rennert, too, lowered his voice, "If you hear it again, you'll let me know, Mrs. Earp," he said as he arose.

"Of course, Mr. Rennert," she answered, as her eyes met his.

Rennert walked slowly down the aisle, sensing as he did so the tenseness of the atmosphere that prevailed in the ear. (Like, he thought grimly, a bunch of mice watching a cat.)

Mrs. Willis reached past her husband and caught his sleeve. Her eyes were red and little lines about her lips and cheeks had aged her face, softening at the same time its hardness.

"Oh, Mr. Rennert," she breathed as he leaned toward her, "this is terrible! To know that that poor man was strangled with those hose and that it was our fault. Do you still think the man who did it is in this car?"

"Yes, Mrs. Willis," Rennert said gravely, "I do. But you had best not worry—"

"But how can I help it, Mr. Renner?" her voice rose. "What if he should think one of us knows who he is and decide to murder us? What's to keep him from it?"

Rennert's voice was reassuring. "The car is guarded, Mrs. Willis, there is no danger."

"But there is,—oh, I know there is!" her voice rang in his ears as he turned away. (Damn the woman for voicing the fear that kept nagging at him with irritating persistence, like an abscessed tooth which, even when anesthetized, never lets its presence be forgotten.)

He passed Miss McCool and Miss Dean, in low-voiced colloquy with Tancel; Colonel Enloe, sitting erect by the window, his attention seemingly absorbed by the scenery; he smiled pleasantly at Miss Tredkin, who stared at him with frightened eyes and drew away perceptibly as he approached; he paused at the rear seat, where Professor Bymaster sat with averted eyes.

He dropped into the seat opposite the little man and was conscious of a swift withdrawing, not of the body, but of personality into some inner recess. Bymaster's eyes loomed like enormous, expressionless marbles behind the rims of his glasses.

"Good morning, Dr. Bymaster."

"Good morning, Mr. Rennert." His voice was fretful, nervous.

"I want to talk to you, doctor." (He was speaking to a shell, out of which two goggle-eyes peered at him disconcertingly.)

"Yes?"

"I should like very much to examine your bedroom slippers."

He felt as if an opera-glass were being focused against his face.

"Assuredly, Mr. Rennert."

Bymaster leaned forward and opened a brown grip on the seat beside Rennert. (From the handle, Rennert noticed, dangled a red tag.) His hands rummaged in it for a moment and came out holding a pair of odd-looking slippers.

Rennert took them, glanced at them curiously.

The outer surface was of some kind of untanned leather, the fur turned inward.

"Cat," Professor Bymaster pronounced proudly.

Rennert turned the slippers over and held the soles to the light, examining some faint black smears on the instep.

"Angora," Bymaster said.

Rennert carefully placed the slippers in the grip and closed it.

His foot tapped the edge of the steamer trunk under the other's seat.

"I notice," he said, "that your trunk does not have one of the tags of the 'Inter-America Tours' attached to it."

The light did peculiar things with the goggle-eyes. "But it does, Mr. Rennert."

"It does?" Rennert wondered if he *had* actually shouted.

"Yes, Mr. Rennert, it does. You can see for yourself if you like." He moved over in the seat and crossed his legs.

Rennert leaned forward and pulled the trunk toward him. Attached to the handle was a little round red tag.

Rennert shoved the trunk into place again, stared at it thoughtfully.

"All your luggage, Dr. Bymaster?"

"Yes, two pieces."

Rennert looked up at the placid face opposite him. "How long have you had that trunk tagged?" "Since I joined this party in St. Louis." Rennert's eyes narrowed.

"Suppose," he said, "I were to tell you that that is not true?"

There was a frantic twitching of Bymaster's countenance. One hand fluttered quickly to his pocket, drew out a handkerchief. Its arrival at his nose coincided with the sneeze. He gulped, put the handkerchief back into his pocket.

"What was that, Mr. Rennert?"

"I said: 'Suppose I were to tell you that that is not true?'"

"About the tag?"

"Yes." Rennert was conscious of increasing irritability.

"But it is."

"Yesterday that trunk did not have a tag."

"Oh, no, the tag was not on the trunk then. I did not put it on until this morning."

"But I asked you—"

"And I said: 'Since I joined this party in St. Louis.'"

Rennert felt an almost irresistible desire to get to his feet, to pace the floor. There flashed across his mind the tea-table conversation of Alice with the Dormouse and the Mad Hatter.

"It is clear, is it not?" asked Professor Bymaster.

"I asked you," Rennert found himself repeating, "how long you had had that trunk tagged."

Bymaster adjusted his lips in a smile.

"I thought you said: 'How long have you had that trunk *tag?*'—not '*tagged.*'"

Rennert wanted to kick himself for the inaneness of his "Oh."

"A cold in the head," Professor Bymaster said, "always affects my hearing. Doesn't it yours?"

24
LUNCH

Miss Dean plunged her fork into an avocado.

"I think," she said, "that it must be wonderful to be a detective, Mr. Rennert!"

Rennert, who had had his eyes focused on the cool green fruit, found himself jerked out of his abstraction.

"I hope you don't mind our sitting at your table," Miss Dean went on, "but we do want to know what clews you have found. We," her fork embraced Miss McCool and Tancel, "have thought and thought about last night but we can't remember seeing any man dressed in a long dark cloak and a hat with white plumes and a black mask. I can't see why we didn't notice him. Have you found any clews yet, Mr. Rennert?"

"Listen, Gertie," Tancel leaned across the table, "don't you know that detectives can't tell their clews to anybody? If they did, their value would be lost."

Miss Dean moved a trifle closer to Rennert's side.

"But this is different," she protested, "Mr. Rennert is a friend of ours."

"And we won't tell anybody"; Miss McCool chimed in, "not a soul."

Rennert, conscious that the diner had become very still, lowered his voice and said: "Tomorrow" very melodramatically.

"I'm going to help you, Mr. Rennert," Miss Dean announced in a stage whisper which, Rennert was sure, carried to the end of the car. "I've always thought that I could be a detective and I've read lots and lots of detective stories. But, since you're not going to let me in on your secrets, I'm not going to let you in on mine. That is, not until I've solved the case. Then I'll tell you and let you arrest the murderer and get all the credit, like happens in books."

Miss McCool snickered loudly.

"Gertrude Dean, Detective! How are you going about it, Gertie?"

Miss Dean imitated Rennert's enigmatic "Tomorrow!"

"Better stick to your books, Gertie," Tancel laughed.

"I'll bet," her round face became very serious, "that I know things right now about every member of this party that not even Mr. Rennert knows!"

"For instance?" Tancel's eyes were sparkling with merriment over a glass of water.

"I could tell him something about you, all right, Francis. Something that he'd be glad to know."

Tancel put down the glass of water very suddenly.

His fingers closed upon the stem.

"You little—"

Miss McCool's burst of laughter checked him. "Now, now, children," she laid a hand upon his arm, "don't fight. Gertie's not going to tell anything."

Tancel raised the glass to his lips again, drained it slowly.

"She'd better not," he said, as he set it down.

Rennert cleared his throat.

"Don't you think," he suggested, "that we had better go back in the other car? I think everyone is through now."

They got up.

"Wait and see," Miss Dean called over her shoulder to him as she moved toward the door. "I'm going to start looking for clews right now."

Rennert stood aside until they had all left the diner—the Willises and the Earps in one group; Miss Tredkin (her face was cruelly weathered chalk), Brody, Enloe and Bymaster in another;

Argudin, smiling as ever as he passed; Dr. Lipscomb, only shreds of his composure left.

Mrs. Rankin followed them slowly down the aisle. Her calm smile was to Rennert a welcome sight after those tight, drawn faces, carefully composed to hide emotion.

"I am praying for you, Mr. Rennert," she murmured as she passed him.

"Thank you, Mrs. Rankin."

He fell in behind her.

"And for some poor soul among us," the words came softly to his cars, over the rumble of the wheels as they emerged from the diner.

In the other car he stopped and sat for a moment on the arm of her chair.

Mrs. Earp's shrill voice behind him ("Oh, I've lost my scarf!") was an echo of another world as he watched Mrs. Rankin's fragile old fingers pick up the long old-fashioned knitting needles and resume an interrupted stitch.

"Last night," he asked quietly, "did he come?" (She was at work upon something very soft, very fleecy, very white.)

Still smiling, she looked up into his eyes. "No—but I know that he wanted to. Perhaps next year—on the Day of the Dead—he will come."

25
A SCARF IS LOST

RENNERT STOOD UPON the rear platform of the Pullman and tore into bits the telegram which had been handed in to him at the little station. He watched the fragments of paper as they were caught in the swift air of the train's passing and tossed about in mad gyrations for a few seconds before settling to earth far behind. Like, he reflected, his eyes narrowed against the glare of the sun, those people in the Pullman ahead—separate entities caught and whirled by circumstance into elements as strange and as terrifying to their commonplace lives as that wild onrush of air must be to those bits of paper suddenly loosed into space. Tomorrow they would touch earth again, settle again into contact with stable, familiar elements. Except one.

Rennert walked slowly back into the Pullman.

The atmosphere of restraint and tension which had prevailed during the morning seemed to have relaxed. The Willises and Brody were sleeping. Dr. Lipscomb was talking to Mrs. Rankin, whose fingers thrust the long knitting needles in and out, in and out, with movements as soothingly monotonous as the steady hum of the rails beneath them. Miss McCool and Tancel sat side by side, gazing at the landscape and carrying on a low-voiced conversation. Miss Tredkin and Professor Bymaster were reading.

150

Argudin sat as before, staring out the window with expressionless eyes.

The Earps, Miss Dean and Colonel Enloe were playing bridge.
Miss Dean hailed Rennert as he came down the aisle.

"Come on, Mr. Rennert, and take my hand. I'm just quitting,"
she said as he protested. "Got business to attend to. How's the score?"

Earp finished a rapid calculation. "We lost that rubber."

"My partner," Mrs. Earp smiled across the table at Colonel
Enloe, "is *such* a wonderful player."

Rennert sank into the seat which Miss Dean had occupied and
watched Enloe shuffle the cards with quick, deft fingers, while Earp
tore a sheet from the score pad and headed new columns.

"Where did you learn to play bridge so marvelously, Colonel?"
Mrs. Earp asked, her lisp at its best as she slowly released the syllables of the adverb.

"I played quite a bit in the army." Enloe was dealing the cards
with a detached air.

Rennert, with a queer uneasiness, had watched Miss Dean as
she walked resolutely down the aisle, paused for a brief interchange
of words with Miss McCool and Tancel, and sat down beside Miss
Tredkin, who laid aside her magazine and regarded the girl uncertainly as she plunged at once into what seemed an exciting mono-
logue. He saw Miss Tredkin's tight lips become even tighter. She
shook her head several times. (Suppose the girl blundered into
something, threatened someone's fancied security with her fiction-
inspired sleuthing? Of course nothing could happen to her in this
compact, guarded car. . . .)

Colonel Enloe swept his cards together, tapped the edge of the
little pack briskly against the top of the table, like a call to arms,
and arranged them swiftly.

"Two spades," he snapped.

After a brief skirmish, he emerged victorious with the bid at
three spades.

The game was fast and played with a deadly precision. Colonel
Enloe sat erect, his eyes moving quickly from his hand to the board.

He played his cards without hesitation, placing them in the exact center of the table before releasing them. His finesses were daring, but of an uncanny accuracy. Mrs. Earp's game was a slower, more exuberant one, punctuated with exclamations and frequent hesitancy. She showed, however, a thorough grasp of the principles of the game and invariably read her partner's wishes as to the lead. Earp sat slumped down in the seat, his beret aslant, and regarded the play through seemingly indifferent eyes partially covered by drawn lids. He had a habit of flipping his cards onto the board with a little movement of the thumb and forefinger. Rennert saw at once that, of them all, Earp had the best card sense.

Colonel Enloe made his three spade bid without difficulty.

Rennert, as he shuffled the cards, let his eyes wander over the car. Brody had awakened and joined Miss Tredkin and Miss Dean. His broad red face wore a serious expression as he listened to Miss Dean.

Mrs. Earp jostled the table as she leaned over and scrutinized the floor.

"I'm still looking," she said, "for that scarf of mine. I don't know what could have become of it."

Rennert's fingers continued to deal the cards.

"When did you see your scarf last, Mrs. Earp?" he asked.

"Just before lunch. It was hanging here on that hook. And now it's gone."

"What was it like?"

"A long green silk one—one of my wedding presents and I wouldn't lose it for the world." Her lips rounded in a little pout. "Ed says I'm always losing things, but this wasn't my fault, I know."

"Probably one of the trainmen came in and got it while we were out—or maybe one of those soldiers," Enloe suggested. "They're all thieves, these Mexicans."

"But what," Mrs. Earp's fat fingers were picking up her cards, "would a man want with a silk scarf? He couldn't wear it, you know."

"Two no trump," Rennert said.

He looked up as Brody came down the aisle and stopped between them and Dr. Lipscomb.

"What station is this we're getting into?" the big man asked.

"Querétaro," the conductor's voice was animated. "It's an interesting old place. Maximilian was shot here."

"Oh!" Mrs. Earp threw down her cards, "I want to get a look at this place. Let's go out on the observation platform."

Colonel Enloe nudged Rennert's side. Rennert saw him draw toward him the loose sheet from the bridge pad and scribble a few words on the back.

The Frisco runs through Kansas, he read. He smiled and nodded as he followed Enloe's eyes to the black and red time-table which protruded from the pocket of Brody's coat.

Mrs. Earp was on her feet.

"Come on, let's go out on the platform."

They got up and moved toward the rear.

Before he went down the aisle Rennert turned and picked up from the table the sheet from the bridge pad upon which Colonel Enloe had written. He folded it carefully and slipped it into his billfold.

26
SMOOTH AND FRAGILE SILK

RENNERT SANK WEARILY onto the leather cushion of the smoker and watched the scattered lights of San Luis Potosí being slowly engulfed by the darkness.

Another mile-post, he felt, safely past in this curious race. For he had begun to think of it as exactly that—a race, with its goal a narrow stream of water across which this train would carry them on the morrow. By that time he would have the threads of this case (each individual concerned was a thread, twisted and contorted by evasion and his own interests) untangled and his growing conviction would become certainty. If only the journey continued uneventful, if only those forces which he knew lay smoldering beneath the surface remained pent up until the border were safely passed. . . .

Rennert was lighting a cigarette when the green curtains parted abruptly and Professor Bymaster entered.

He nodded in Rennert's direction and walked, his feet shuffling the odd slippers across the floor, to the glass door in the wall. He tried the handle, shook it several times and turned to Rennert.

"Conveniences on trains," he said petulantly, "are not in proportion to those using them."

Rennert tossed the match into the cuspidor and agreed with him.

Bymaster began to walk up and down the room, his hands thrust into the pockets of a faded dressing gown.

"I see," he said, wheeling in front of Rennert, "that you are looking at my slippers."

Rennert nodded.

"I once suffered with gout," Bymaster announced to the glass door.

Rennert uttered a commiserating monosyllable.

"The fur of the cat is said to have peculiar electric qualities." He shook the handle of the door again. "One of my students knew of my affliction and presented me with these slippers. He thought that the vibrations from the fur of the cat might have a beneficial effect on my feet. When this cat died of old age he had a shoemaker make this pair of slippers out of the skin—pelt, I believe he called it."

The door opened and Tancel emerged.

"I no longer have gout," Bymaster said as he made for the door.

Tancel smiled pleasantly at Rennert.

"Any news?" he asked, splashing his hands in the water of the basin.

"Not yet."

"You've got an assistant now, I hear." Tancel reached for a towel. "Gertie Dean.'

"Yes," Rennert laughed.

"Say," Tancel said, facing Rennert and rubbing his hands briskly with the towel, "you didn't pay any attention to what she said out there in the diner this noon, did you? About her knowing something about me, I mean?"

Rennert smiled impersonally.

"I think," he said, "that I know what she knows."

"Oh!" Tancel's eyes fell. He folded the towel carefully, twisted it back and forth through his nervous fingers.

"About the grip?" he asked softly.

"Yes."

"Did she tell you?"

"No. I searched your room yesterday."

"Oh!" Tancel wadded the towel into a ball and tossed it into the receptacle. He smiled as he looked at Rennert. "In that case, I'd better get busy."

"Yes," Rennert smiled back at him, "you'd better get busy. We cross the border at two o'clock tomorrow."

At the doorway Tancel paused, one hand on the green curtains, the other running lightly through his tousled hair.

"Thanks," he said.

The curtains fell to behind him.

Rennert continued to smile as he tossed his cigarette from him. It struck the edge of the cuspidor and fell to the floor. He leaned forward and crushed it with his shoe. His shoe became suddenly motionless as he stared at an object which protruded from the crack between the end of the cushion and the window. He reached out his hand, but withdrew it quickly as Colonel Enloe came into the room.

"Good evening, Rennert." Enloe walked to a basin and deposited a traveling kit. "I'm turning in early. That party last night was too much for me. Guess I'm getting old."

He tried the handle of the glass door and turned away.

"Today has been rather a strain on all of us, I'm afraid," Rennert said.

"Yes," Enloe removed his shirt and tossed it at a hook, "I'll be glad when we get across the line." He bent over the basin. His hands threw water against his face with the wholesale efficiency of a seal's flappers.

"So," Rennert said, "shall I."

He was looking at the bare pink shoulder turned toward him. Across it, from the top halfway to the elbow, ran a long livid scar. Yesterday, in Enloe's room at the hotel, it had been barely noticeable. Now it was a daub of scarlet against the healthy pink flesh.

"Bad looking scar you have there," Rennert commented.

Enloe was rubbing his face and neck to a ruddy glow.

"Oh, that," he laughed, "it's an old one. Not as bad as it looks."

Professor Bymaster came out, his lips pressed tightly together. He glanced sharply at Enloe without speaking and washed his hands in a basin in the corner.

"Patience," he announced as he went through the curtains at the door, "is a great virtue particularly in the use of the conveniences on a train."

Enloe, oblivious of the Parthian shot directed against him, was standing before the door, his left shoulder turned toward the mirror.

"I got that," he said, "in an accident on the Irrawaddy River, years ago. It never healed very well. I must have bruised it on something last night."

He took a toothbrush and a tube of paste from his kit and turned his back on Rennert.

"If you want to know the details about the Irrawaddy affair, you can get them from that red-headed schoolmarm," he said indistinctly.

Rennert, whose imagination had taken the bit in its teeth and was headed for dimly seen plague-spots of the East where devotees of Kali coiled silken ropes, sternly pulled at the reins.

"How's that?" he asked.

Enloe's laugh was a guttural sound through tooth paste.

"She's been pumping me for all my history—past, present and future. She asked me a while ago what my reactions, as an ex-army man, were toward the taking of human life. The gal's crazy as a loon."

Rennert watched Enloe finish his ablutions and put on his shirt. He was thinking about Miss Dean. He was wanting to be bromidic and quote something about fools rushing in where angels feared to tread.

"Well," the colonel said, picking up his kit, "I'm going to bed. See you in the morning, Rennert."

"Good night, Colonel."

Rennert sat very still until the sound of the heavy footsteps had died away in the passage. Then he leaned quickly down and drew from the recess behind the cushion Mrs. Earp's silk scarf. His face was grave as he slipped it into the pocket of his coat.

Twice, he admitted to himself, he had been afraid during this case. Both times something had happened so strange that it hovered for a moment on the borders of the inexplicable.

There had been that terrible moment last night when he had realized that the accuracy of his aim with the revolver availed nothing against that dark figure advancing toward his bed.

And now this piece of silk that felt so smooth and fragile against his fingers. . . .

27
IN THE PASSAGE

THE TROPIC OF CANCER, MIDNIGHT.
TO LAREDO, 615 KILOMETERS

RENNERT SUDDENLY SAT UP very straight in his berth.

Beneath him the contact of iron against iron assumed in the stillness of the night the gentle soothing rhythm of a lullaby.

But Rennert was very much awake.

He slipped his feet from under the covers and sat on the edge of the berth. He listened and heard it again—the soft shuffle of slippered feet in the corridor outside.

He got quickly to his feet and put on his dressing gown and slippers. Into a pocket he thrust his automatic and moved on tiptoe to the door. He opened it, glanced down the dimly illuminated aisle, blanketed now by gently billowing green curtains, and rounded the corner into the narrow corridor at the rear.

The curtains at the doorway of the smoker were pushed violently apart and a tall figure rushed out. He stepped back to avoid the threatened collision and his hand closed about the automatic.

There was a gasp, compounded of fright and anger and outraged virginal emotions, and he recognized Miss Tredkin.

One hand clutched a kimono over the front of a long white nightgown, the other was clapped over her mouth. Her eyes, seen without spectacles and under a white nightcap, were the wildly frantic ones of a trapped creature's.

For one startled moment they stood and stared at each other. Then another cry filtered through her fingers and she moved in headlong flight down the corridor.

Rennert stepped aside to let her pass.

"I made a mistake!" The words reached his ears indistinctly as the white nightcap disappeared around the corner.

28
THE KNITTING NEEDLE

MONTERREY, 8:00 A.M.
TO LAREDO, 269 KILOMETERS

RENNERT STEPPED ONTO the platform of the station at Monterrey and glanced about him. His eyes lighted at the sight of a tall spare man in shirt and trousers of olive drab, who was making his way toward him through the rapidly dispersing crowd.

"Hello, Johnston."

"Hello, Rennert."

They shook hands and walked toward the rear of the car.

"Going to the border with us?" Rennert asked.

"No, not this trip. Unless you need me, that is. I was to meet you here and find out how things were going. And to give you this," he took a heavy buff envelope from his pocket and gave it to Rennert. "It came up from Mexico City by airplane yesterday."

"Good," Rennert carefully put the envelope in the inner pocket of his coat. "That, I hope, will cinch the case."

"Say," the other's voice was discreetly low as he cupped his hands about a match and applied it to a cigarette, "you're rather getting out of your line, aren't you? This is a murder case, I understand."

"It is now. Originally it was quite different."

"What's the dope on it? Some kind of smuggling, isn't it?"

"Yes, a new racket—or rather an old, old one conducted on a businesslike, wholesale basis.

"For years we've known that expeditions and individuals engaged in excavation work in the ancient Mexican ruins were secretly bringing stuff into the United States. Most of it found its way to museums—idols, old pottery, jewelry, masks and so forth. You probably remember the trouble when it was discovered that the Sacred Well of Chichen Itza had been dredged secretly by a former North American consular officer and a number of rare objects taken out of the country.

"All this came into the United States in dribbles, however, and most of it wasn't of much intrinsic value—stone, obsidian, bone and non-precious material like that, so nothing was ever done about it.

"Since the Revolution the Mexican government has awakened to the fact that they are letting foreigners take out of the country most of their great archeological treasures. There was quite a furor about a certain incident down in Taxco and for a time they closed down on it rather tight."

They turned and walked back toward the train. Rennert took off his hat and ran his fingers through his hair.

"About a year ago," he continued, "they began to suspect that, far from having stopped, this contraband trade had been systematized and was being conducted on a wholesale basis from a central point. Museums in the United States were adding to their Mexican collections steadily. It was suspected that a great deal of gold and precious jewels was finding its way to the regular jewelry trade. Several times, mounds which had been thought to be untouched for centuries were found to contain tombs which had been rifled recently. In regular excavation sites, when work was resumed after the rainy season, it was found that pirating had been carried on on a large scale.

"Several American artists and explorers resident in Mexico were suspected of conducting this work, but nothing was ever proven against them. Finally the Mexican government protested to the United States government and, since a great deal of the stuff which is going into the country now is dutiable, it came into our line. Young Payne was put onto it and worked for months along the border and in Mexico. He finally got onto the trail of the person who was financing the business—buying up stuff from agents in Mexico, shipping it into the United States by various routes and selling it to museums and private collectors. Our last communication from Payne was to the effect that this person was making regular trips back and forth across the border as a member of tourist parties.

"Payne believed that he was in this group," Rennert jerked a thumb in the direction of the Pullman ahead, "and was going to join them too and try to get some evidence against him. He was murdered before the party left San Antonio."

Ahead the bell of the engine jangled warningly. Rennert and his companion walked quickly toward the steps.

"And you've got the murderer in that car?"

Rennert nodded.

"Any proof?"

Rennert paused with one foot on the lower step and tapped his breast pocket.

"I think," he said, "that this will be the proof."

Rennert walked along the corridor, his mind on breakfast.

Halfway down its length he met Dr. Lipscomb, his face pale and worn, but his lips retaining their bland smile.

"Good morning, Mr. Rennert," he said. "May we not eat breakfast now?"

"Yes. Everybody up?"

"Everybody, I think, except Miss Dean."

"Except Miss Dean?" Rennert repeated sharply.

"Yes, she seems to be sleeping late."

Dr. Lipscomb turned and preceded Rennert down the passage.

Just as they were about to round the corner, both men stopped, riveted for an instant in their places by the shrill cry of terror which beat against their ears.

Rennert shoved Dr. Lipscomb to one side and ran into the Pullman.

The members of the party were huddled in two little groups, one at each end of the car, while Miss McCool stood in the aisle before the one unmade berth and screamed again and again, in a high, hysteric note, like the sound that a phonograph needle makes when stuck in a groove.

Rennert pushed through the group in the aisle and pulled aside the curtains of the unmade lower berth.

Below the lowered blind a wavering beam of sunlight entered and fell full upon Miss Dean's body, shapelessly inert in bright purple pajamas, upon the reddish copper of her hair, and upon the knobbed end of a long steel knitting needle which protruded from a sticky-looking patch of red dampness at her breast.

29
THE NOTEBOOK

Monterrey, 8:25 a.m.
To Laredo, 269 kilometers

For an instant, as he stood with his back to the closed curtains of that berth, Rennert felt blind anger sweep over him in a wave—anger at the wretched futility of this girl's death, anger at himself for his negligence, anger at the tall figure in blue which stood before him and screamed and screamed in insane repetition.

With both hands he grasped Miss McCool's shoulders and shook her with all his force. She lost her balance, a dazed expression came over her face, and he caught her as she toppled forward in his arms.

He laid her on the seat opposite and turned to the white-faced Tancel, who stood near by.

"Get some water," he said.

The young man turned down the aisle and Rennert faced the others.

"Sit down," he ordered, surprised himself at the steadiness of his voice.

He watched them as they sank into the nearest seats—Mrs. Willis, emitting dry sobs that shook her body convulsively as she buried her face against her husband's shoulder; Mrs. Rankin, staring at him through a pale, expressionless mask; Mrs. Earp, her eyes two blue slits in a white face as she plucked with frantic fingers at her husband's sleeve, which he had passed protectively about her shoulders; Enloe, sitting erect in his seat and giving evidence of his emotion only by a slight flush on his cheeks and by the manner in which he chewed the end of his mustache; Miss Tredkin, standing upright and pulling a handkerchief to shreds with jerky mechanical movements of her fingers, while Brody, red of face and a look of bewilderment in his eyes, attempted to pull her down into the seat beside him; Bymaster, clasping and unclasping his hands as he stared glassily at Rennert over the back of a seat; Argudin, sitting very, very still on the rear seat and running the tip of a red tongue over his full, red lips.

Tancel lurched down the aisle and went on his knees before Miss McCool, holding to her lips a paper cup.

An ugly calm settled over the car, broken only by Mrs. Willis' low sobbing.

"Miss Dean," Rennert said, "is dead—"

He caught a gasp from Miss Tredkin as she sank onto the seat.

"One of you," he continued, his eyes passing slowly around the little group, "murdered her. It was a senseless, cruel thing to do— the act of a beast. You, the one of you who did it, need expect no mercy now."

Mrs. Willis' low sobbing paused for an instant, then resumed again, in maddening monotone Rennert looked at Mrs. Rankin.

"She was stabbed," he said, "with one of your knitting needles."

Mrs. Rankin winced and her eyes closed for an instant. Then she was looking at him again, outwardly calm, but breathing in slow, labored gasps.

"When did you last see that knitting needle, Mrs. Rankin?"

Her voice seemed to ring out clearly in the hushed atmosphere of the car. "Last night, when I went to bed, about ten o'clock. My knitting and my needles were in my workbag. I put it in the upper berth. I took the bag down this morning, but did not open it until just now. The needles are not there now. There were two of them, you know."

"Did you hear anyone moving about during the night?"

She shook her head. "No, I slept soundly and heard nothing."

"Did any one of you," Rennert looked from face to face, "hear or see anyone pass by Mrs. Rankin's berth last night after ten o'clock? Did any one of you hear or see anyone near this berth last night?"

No one spoke.

"Miss Tredkin, you went down this aisle last night at midnight. Did you hear or see anyone else?"

Her face went very white, then very red. She moved her bloodless lips, but no sound came from them. She shook her head.

Tancel stood up and faced Rennert.

"I heard someone sneeze during the night," he said.

"Where?"

"Down that way," he pointed to the rear of the ear. "I don't know what time it was, but it must have been late. It sounded loud and distinct, like someone was in the aisle."

Rennert saw Tancel's eyes go to Professor Bymaster's face.

"It sounded," he said, "like you."

Professor Bymaster stared dazedly at the speaker.

"Did you," Rennert demanded of him, "go down this aisle last night after ten o'clock?"

"Yes," Bymaster said, in a hoarse, strained voice, "I believe I did."

"Where did you go?"

The little man's Adam's apple shot up and down above his stiff white collar.

"To the bathroom," he said. It was almost a whisper.

"Did you hear or see anyone about?"

"No! No! No one."

"What time was it?"

"I do not know. I did not consult my watch. I know nothing—"

Miss McCool got slowly to her feet. Her face looked old and haggard and her eyes seemed to have sunk into her head. She pushed back a straggling lock of hair.

"One of you damn cowards killed Gertie," she said huskily, her breast rising and falling, "but you're not going to get away with it!" her voice rose, "you're not going to get away with it, do you hear?" Her eyes met Rennert's. "Will you," she asked, "look under her pillow and get that little notebook?"

He looked at her for a moment, then turned and lifted the green curtain. His hand fumbled under the pillow and closed about an object which he found there. He brought it forth. It was a small stenographer's notebook.

"That's it!" Miss McCool cried. "Now—"

Rennert slipped the book in his pocket and caught her arm.

"I think," he said quietly, "that we had better look at this in the drawing-room."

30
HOOKS AND CURVES

MORALES, 9:24 A.M.
TO LAREDO, 226 KILOMETERS

MISS McCOOL PUT DOWN her coffee cup and leaned back in her chair. She accepted and lit the cigarette which Rennert offered her. Her face, as she watched the smoke dribbling from her mouth, was washed-out looking and there were drawn lines about the corners of her lips and eyes. In those eyes, however, determination burned fiercely.

"Now," she asked, "can I talk?"

He nodded.

"You remember," she said slowly, "that Gertie was talking at lunch yesterday about going to do some detective work and find out which one of that bunch in there was the one you were looking for.

"Well, she spent all afternoon talking to different ones. I just laughed at her and kidded her about trying to be a sleuth. Last night, though, when I was getting ready to go to bed, I looked in her berth. She was writing in a notebook. I asked her what she was doing and she said that she was arranging the notes of her day's work," she smiled weakly. "She said that she had gotten a lot of information about the people in this party that you had probably never suspected. Said she was jotting down every detail in shorthand and that today she would study it over.

"Mr. Rennert," Miss McCool leaned forward and her eyes narrowed, "Gertie got onto something yesterday! And because she did, someone murdered her last night. And you'll find the reasons why she was murdered in that notebook."

Rennert drew the book from his pocket and glanced through its pages.

"Did anyone besides yourself know about this notebook?" he asked, without looking up.

"No. Not a soul."

"Do you read shorthand, Miss McCool?"

"No. Say, that's right, isn't it? We'll have to get someone to read it for us."

"I think," Rennert said, "that that can be arranged."

He closed the book and slipped it into his pocket again.

She arose.

"I believe," she glanced at herself in the mirror, "that some powder and lipstick would help me."

Rennert got to his feet and held the door open for her.

"Thank you, Miss McCool."

She paused for an instant and steadied herself against his arm.

"Poor Gertie," she said, as if to herself, "always so happy and cheerful! Never had a serious thought in the world."

31
MRS. EARP READS SHORTHAND

RENNERT STOOD in the center of the drawing-room and surveyed the sheeted figure which lay so still in his berth, whither he had had it moved. Then he went out, closing the door softly behind him.

The occupants of the Pullman sat in white-faced expectancy at the front and rear of the car, as far as possible from that still un-made, yet empty berth in the center.

He faced them, holding in his right hand the notebook.

"Does anyone here," he asked, "read shorthand?"

There was silence for a moment in the car, then Mrs. Earp said weakly:

"I used to, Mr. Rennert."

Rennert walked down the aisle to her side.

"I wonder," he asked, handing her the book, "if you could read this for me? It contains Miss Dean's notes."

For an instant she hesitated, seemed about to let the book fall from her fingers. Then she opened it, glanced at the first page.

"I think so," her voice was barely audible, "I'll try. I'll have to study it over a while, though. I've forgotten so much, you see."

"Thank you, Mrs. Earp. Let me know when you have read it."

32
THE LAST PAGE

JARITA, 1: 26 P.M.
TO LAREDO, 29 KILOMETERS

"AND NOW," Rennert said quietly, "I am going to ask Mrs. Earp to read the shorthand notes which Miss Dean wrote last night."

Mrs. Earp rose unsteadily to her feet, nibbling at the edge of a bedraggled lace handkerchief. The hand which held the brown notebook was trembling violently.

Rennert let his glance wander over the faces turned toward him.

They sat, all of them, at the rear of the car. To his left, Dr. Lipscomb and Professor Bymaster, both very still and intent-looking; to his right, Earp, leaning back and regarding him through lazy half-closed eyes, his feet propped upon the seat opposite; Mrs. Rankin, her clear eyes resting on Rennert's face, her fingers playing abstractedly with something very pink and soft-looking, as if in lieu of the knitting needles to which they were accustomed; beside her, her head still for once and her lips held very firmly, Miss McCool; Tancel, seated upon the arm of the seat, his mouth grim and set; the Willises, their faces pale and expressionless, as if from sheer exhaustion; Brody and Miss Tredkin and, opposite them, Enloe, his head half turned to Rennert; behind them, Argudin, a sleepy, torpid expression in his dark eyes and a trace of a smile at the corners of his lips. His teeth, seen through half-parted lips, were very white and pearly and firm-looking.

Rennert's eyes met Mrs. Earp's.

"All right," he said, "we are ready."

The lace handkerchief fell to the floor as Mrs. Earp grasped the book with both hands.

"The first page," she began in a low voice, "is headed 'Francis Tancel'—"

Rennert saw the young man stir uneasily and cross his legs. The fingers of his right hand held an unlighted cigarette, which he was slowly crumbling to bits.

Mrs. Earp suddenly squared her shoulders and her voice, even and incisive, sifted clearly through the stillness:

"'Mr. Rennert knows about the false bottom in his grip that he was going to use to carry liquor across the border—'" (Rennert's eyes met Tancel's for an instant and he smiled at the faint flush which spread over the young man's cheeks) "'but he does not know about the night of October twenty-seventh, when we were in the Patio Hotel in San Antonio. After Argudin left to get some cigarettes Jo and I went up to our rooms. We were gone about five minutes. Francis was in the cardroom when we left and when we got back, but he could have had time to get to the fourth floor, where that Mr. Payne roomed, and back again by the time we did.'"

Mrs. Earp paused and turned a page.

"I did not leave the cardroom," Tancel said evenly. His eyes looked straight into Rennert's. "I thought that as long as the girls didn't mention the fact that they had gone upstairs I wasn't going to say anything about it. Do you believe me?"

"Yes," Rennert said, "I believe you. You did not leave the cardroom."

Tancel gave a little sigh of relief and settled back against the seat.

"Thanks," he said, "and the false bottom of my grip is empty now."

"All right, Mrs. Earp," Rennert turned to her, "you may go on."

"The second page," she said, "is short. It's about Mr. and Mrs. Willis—and a luggage tag."

"What!"

The exclamation seemed to come involuntarily from Willis' lips as he sat bolt upright in his seat.

"Yes," Mrs. Earp went on. "This is what Miss Dean wrote:

"'On the train on the way down Mr. Willis had an extra luggage tag. I saw it in his pocketbook one day on the diner when he was paying his check. I do not think that Mr. Rennert knows about this.'"

"Is that true, Mr. Willis?" Rennert asked.

"Yes," Willis spoke resignedly, "it's true. I had forgotten all about it. You remember that I told you that one of our bags had been left at home," he glanced quickly at his wife out of the corner of his eye. "When we met Dr. Lipscomb at the station in St. Louis he asked me how many pieces of luggage we had. I told him three. I did not know then that we had forgotten the other bag. When we discovered it, I put the tags on the two pieces and stuck the other tag in my pocketbook. I remember seeing it there at the border when I got my money changed and threw it away." He gestured wearily with his hand. "That's all."

Silence fell upon the car.

"Shall I go on, Mr. Rennert?" Mrs. Earp asked.

"Yes," he said. "I do not think that we shall have to trouble Mr. Willis again."

"The third page," Mrs. Earp said, "is headed: 'Colonel Enloe' and there's a question mark after his name."

Rennert let his eyes follow the others' to Colonel Enloe's face. Seen in profile there was a metallic fixity about its sharp outlines. The only indication of emotion was the tip of a very red tongue which was running over dry lips.

"Oh!" the cry came from Miss Tredkin, "the train has stopped."

The sudden cessation of the steady hum of the rails left a vacuum-like sensation in the car, as if they had been falling and were abruptly suspended motionless in midair. Heat closed in upon them heavily.

"Yes," Rennert said, "we are at the border. We cross in a few minutes."

Dr. Lipscomb made as if to arise from his seat. "But the baggage," he said, "it must be inspected."

Rennert waved him back.

"That formality, Dr. Lipscomb, will be dispensed with this time. I have already inspected the baggage."

The conductor sank back upon the seat and passed a handkerchief over his damp forehead

"You may continue reading, Mrs. Earp."

"'I have put a question mark after Colonel Enloe's name because I do not think that that is his right one.'" (Mrs. Earp's voice, in the stillness, seemed unpleasantly loud and strained.) "'The other day, while I was sitting in the lobby of the hotel I saw Colonel Enloe stop at the cigar counter to buy a cigar. A man—he looked like an American but was dark and tanned—came up to the counter. He looked at Colonel Enloe for a minute as if he was trying to remember him. Then he struck him on the shoulder and held out his hand. He said: "Why, I'll be damned if it isn't Guy Murchison!" Colonel Enloe turned round as if he had been shot and whispered something to the man. I could not hear what it was. They went off together. I think that Mr. Rennert should look into Colonel Enloe's past. It probably is a shady one.'" Mrs. Earp paused and looked inquiringly at Rennert. "That's all on that page. Shall I go on?"

"Just a minute!" Colonel Enloe was standing in the center of the aisle, his arms folded. His jaw was thrust forward belligerently and his cold blue eyes were fixed on Rennert's face.

"Yes, Colonel Enloe?" Rennert looked at him steadily.

"That damn girl was right—my name isn't Enloe. It's Murchison—Guy Murchison." His eyes went to the window. "We are about to cross the river?"

"Yes, Murchison, we are about to cross the river."

"Good! Then there is no reason why I should not tell you why I changed my name when I came down here."

His voice fell slightly. "I was formerly a colonel in the United States Army—that is correct. I saw service along the border and was with the Punitive Expedition that went into Mexico after Villa. A few years after that I was in a saloon in a border town—it doesn't matter now which one. I got in a dispute with a Mexican and struck him over the head with a bottle. I was with some friends and they got me back across the border. Later, it developed that this Mexican was a high official in the state, with lots of influence. He died.

There was a big commotion raised over it and I resigned from the army—partly because my health had not been good and, since I had come into a little bit of money, I wanted to rest and take things easy for a while.

"I have wanted to go to Mexico City for a long time but was always afraid that I'd get in trouble if I went across the border. So I finally decided to use another name and try it. I didn't think that anyone would recognize me after all these years. The man Miss Dean heard speak to me was in the army when I was and knew me, of course, by the name of Murchison."

"But the tourist certificate which I secured for you!" Dr. Lipscomb looked at him and frowned.

The other laughed. "That was easy. I had three of my friends write letters of identification for Colonel Enloe. That was enough."

His glance met Rennert's. "Any questions you want to ask?"

Rennert shook his head. "I think not, Colonel Murchison."

Murchison sat down heavily and stared out the window.

The sounds of shouting and chattering and the movement of heavy trucks on the platform outside came in to them confusedly, as if from a great distance. They seemed to filter in, without disturbing, the stillness of the car.

"You may go on, Mrs. Earp," Rennert said.

"The next page," she said, "is about Mr. Argudin."

A low laugh came from the rear of the car.

"I wondered if the young lady would neglect me," Argudin's voice had a faint touch of sibilance.

Rennert looked at him and at the white, pearly, firm-looking teeth.

"Go on, Mrs. Earp," he said.

"'I believe that Argudin is a professional cardsharp and that he came on this trip so that he could win money from us.'"

Argudin's laugh was not so low this time.

"I believe," he said, "that this information has been disseminated rather widely among these people."

Mrs. Earp did not look up. "'He is wearing,'" she continued, "'a plaster over his chin. Mr. Rennert says that he struck the man who attacked him with the barrel of his revolver. There is certain to be some trace of the wound. I think that Mr. Rennert should make him tell how he cut his chin.'"

Mrs. Earp grasped the edge of the seat as the train gave a jerk. It came to a standstill again, then with much puffing and after several more ineffectual starts, began to move onward.

Rennert stooped and peered through the window. "We are now," he said quietly, "in United States territory."

"Thank God!" the muttered exclamation (from Brody, it seemed) broke the silence.

"If any one of you has anything to declare," Rennert continued, "he will soon have the opportunity to do so." He was gazing steadily at Argudin.

"Teeth—and their fillings—are sometimes dutiable, I might add."

The pupils of Argudin's eyes contracted slowly. He stared at Rennert for a moment, then laughed silently and shrugged his shoulders.

"*Touché!*" he murmured. "You win, Mr. Rennert. I shall declare the diamonds."

Rennert's smile was pleasant. "It usually pays," he said.

"For God's sake, man," Colonel Murchison burst out impatiently, "have Mrs. Earp finish reading that notebook and let's get this over with!"

"Very well," Rennert glanced at him, then at Mrs. Earp. "Will you continue, Mrs. Earp?"

"Yes."

Her eyes fell to the notebook, then arose to meet Rennert's.

"But that's all there is," she said.

"All there is?"

"Yes."

"May I see the notebook, please?"

She handed it to him.

Rennert glanced at it.

"There's a page torn out here," he said.

"Yes, I noticed that. It is the last page." Rennert closed the notebook and slipped it in his pocket.

His hand, when it came out, held a sheet of paper.

"No matter," he said; "I transcribed it myself this morning."

Their eyes met—his clear and lucent, hers two icy blue slits in a white face.

She steadied herself against the seat.

"Do you read shorthand, Mr. Rennert?" the words came from down in her throat.

"Yes, Mrs. Earp, I read shorthand."

Silence, then:

"Damn you—" her shrill scream beat upon his ears.

Rennert stepped backward quickly and caught her wrists as she came toward him.

At his side there was the sound of a scuffle, a smothered exclamation, and a clatter upon the floor. Rennert turned his head.

Earp stood, with manacled hands, smiling at him. His head was bare and across his forehead was a narrow white bandage. Upon the floor at his feet lay a long steel knitting needle.

Inspector Miles, very big and red-faced and perspiring, stood at Earp's side. At a nod from the inspector another stolid uniformed man stepped forward and approached Mrs. Earp. He looked inquiringly at Rennert.

"Yes," Rennert said, "the accomplice."

The steel cuffs clicked about her wrists.

33
NORTHWARD

INSPECTOR MILES, of the San Antonio police, sat at his ease in the smoking room of the Pullman, rolled a big-bellied cigar around in his mouth with an appreciative tongue, and looked approvingly at Rennert, who sat beside him, likewise savoring the evidence of the Lone Star State's hospitality.

Inspector Miles was telling himself that this proved again his private conviction that he was a judge of men. From the moment he had shaken Rennert's hand, that morning in his office in San Antonio, he had known that here was a reliable man, one who would fulfill any mission he might undertake. That's what he had told his wife, when he had asked her about the silk stockings. He'd said that he wished this Rennert fellow were on the force. There was a rather dreamy look in those brown eyes, of course, but one shouldn't judge a man's character by his eyes. . . .

"Now," he said, taking the cigar from his mouth and knocking off the gray cone of ash, "tell me how you got onto this Earp fellow's racket."

Rennert was gazing past Inspector Miles and out the window, where the flat sands of the Rio Grande lay quivering beneath the afternoon sun.

"The first time," he said (his voice, to Inspector Miles, curiously remote and far-away), "that I suspected that the Earps were not exactly what they pretended to be—a pair of honeymooners—

178

was when we were standing on top of the pyramid of the Sun at Teotihuacan. Mrs. Earp was trying to adjust a pair of field glasses. I noticed that her wedding ring was an old one; the gold was tarnished. It was a little thing and there were several plausible explanations. It might have been a family heirloom, for example.

"But when I examined their room I knew that they had been married much longer than they said. Mrs. Earp's dresses and lingerie were not new and," a smile played about Rennert's lips, "it has always been my understanding that a bride has a trousseau of new things. Her luggage was old and showed signs of wear, but it was stamped with her initials—MJE. In her hatbox was a letter addressed to her, as Mrs. Earp, in Chicago and written in July, during the Olympic Games in Los Angeles. So, when she told me that they had been married the day before they joined Dr. Lipscomb's party, I knew that she was lying—for some reason or other.

"Still, that in itself did not constitute conclusive proof that they were the guilty ones. There was much more suspicious evidence against several other members of the party.

"It was on the Night of the Dead, the night I was attacked, that I began to suspect them seriously. I was called to the telephone in the hall, but when I got there the party calling had gone. The operator informed me that it was a woman who had called. While I was out of the room, someone, probably a tall man in a mask whom I met in the hall, entered, took my key and filled my revolver, a Smith & Wesson .38, with blank cartridges. Later, he let himself in with the key (the room had a spring lock and I didn't notice that the key was missing when I returned from the telephone) and attempted to strangle me. I fired at him and, when he kept coming toward me, I struck him with the barrel of the revolver. This convinced me that the man I was after had an accomplice—a woman— and I had seen in Earp's room a box of blank cartridges, for a Smith & Wesson .38. The rope he had taken from Brody's and Enloe's room."

Rennert glanced at his watch.

"I'll have to hurry over the rest of it," he said. "It's almost time for the train to leave.

"When we left Mexico City I felt sure that Earp was guilty, although I was not sure that I had enough evidence against him to convict him. When Dr. Lipscomb told me that someone had left a note signed with my name, informing him that I was going to stay in Mexico City, I wired back for the note to be sent to me by airplane at Monterrey. It was found in the wastebasket in Lipscomb's room. Earp must have written it and slipped it under Lipscomb's door before he attacked me. He was so confident that I would be dead in the morning and himself on the way to the border before the body was discovered that he did not try to disguise the handwriting when he signed my name to it. It corresponds with his writing of my name on a bridge score which I obtained yesterday.

"Earp knew that I had met him in the hall when I was on my way back to my room from the telephone and, when I inquired about a tall man wearing a mask and a long cape, he and his wife had a ready story about such a man having come to Tancel's room. No one else, however, had seen this man. That the man who attacked me was wearing a costume of some kind, I felt sure, since I had smelled the odor of mothballs while he was in my room.

"In the meantime that girl, Miss Dean, had most foolishly decided to do some detecting on her own score. She found out several things. I'll read you what she wrote."

Rennert drew from his pocket a slip of paper.

"'The Earps have been married a long time. Her lingerie and dresses are old. Her wedding ring is old. They were not as drunk as they pretended to be last night.' That was the night the rope was taken from Brody's room. 'Mr. Rennert says that he struck someone with his gun last night. Earp is wearing a beret pulled down over the right side of his forehead. I reached over his shoulder today and pushed it up. There is a bandage under it.'"

Rennert returned the paper to his pocket.

"That," he said, "signed Miss Dean's death warrant. Earp's suspicions were aroused by her questioning and when he saw that she had seen the bandage under his beret he knew that he must silence her. His preparations were rather clever. He took his wife's silk scarf and hid it in the smoker, in the hope that I or someone else would find it. For a while, after I had found it, I wondered if I had been wrong about the Earps—just as he hoped would be the case. If he intended to use this scarf to strangle anyone, why hide it in the smoker? When Miss Dean's body was discovered, stabbed with the knitting needle, I saw through the trick. I was to think that the murderer had taken the scarf and hidden it in the smoker. When he found it was gone, he had taken the knitting needle from Mrs. Rankin's bag.

"I knew that Mrs. Earp had been a stenographer and so read shorthand. I asked her to read Miss Dean's notes—after having made a copy of them myself. If they were guilty, I knew that she would remove the last page, which concerned them. That is what happened."

Rennert glanced at his watch again.

"We'll probably never know exactly what happened in that hotel in San Antonio. Probably Payne aroused Earp's suspicions in some way. My guess would be," a grim smile was on Rennert's lips, "that he used his wife as a bait, had her go to Payne's room and engage him in conversation. When Earp saw the silk stockings lying on the floor of the hall outside Willis' room he realized that, besides answering his purpose—that of killing Payne noiselessly— they would serve to cast suspicion upon the Willises. He probably thrust them into his pocket, entered Payne's room and strangled him. When he pulled the stockings from his pocket, he dropped the luggage tag which he had there. Dr. Lipscomb, I had learned, had given him an extra one that day, when he bought a new suitcase."

Rennert rose.

"One of the little quirks of life that some people call fate was the murder party game which we played our last night in Mexico City. I feel sure that one of the Earps drew the marked piece of paper and was afraid to attract attention by admitting it." Rennert extended his hand.

"I must say good-by to these people before the train leaves."

Inspector Miles likewise got to his feet and clasped Rennert's hand.

"Good-by, Rennert, see you in San Antonio tomorrow."

Rennert walked into the Pullman, whence proceeded a sound somewhat like that of a beehive, and passed down the aisle, making his farewells.

He shook hands with Dr. Lipscomb, genial and smiling again; with Mrs. Rankin, whose bright eyes looked into his as their hands touched; with the Willises, their equanimity magically restored by contact with United States soil; with Miss McCool and Tancel, still subdued and silent; with Colonel Murchison, who gripped his hand with the words, "Congratulations, Rennert—knew you'd carry it through!"; and with Bymaster, who released his hand to pass his own around a wilting collar. Rennert's fingers had left Argudin's cold damp ones and he had started for the door when Brody called to him.

The big man came up, passed an arm around Rennert's shoulders and whispered something in his ear.

Rennert smiled, his eyes on Miss Tredkin's flushed face.

"Congratulations, Brody!"

A sudden, irresistible impulse swept over him.

Stepping past Brody, he caught Miss Tredkin's thin shoulders and kissed her squarely on the mouth. He turned then and swung to the platform.

As the train moved northward, he stood regarding his handkerchief.

"A hell of a detective," he told himself. "I'd never have suspected that she used lipstick!"

COACHWHIP PUBLICATIONS

COACHWHIPBOOKS.COM

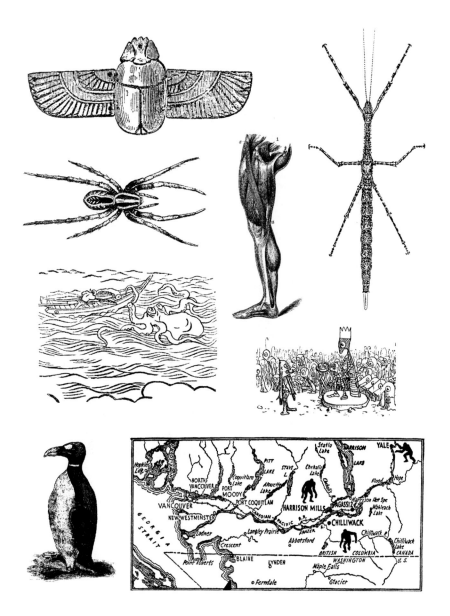

The Cat Screams
ISBN 1-61646-148-9

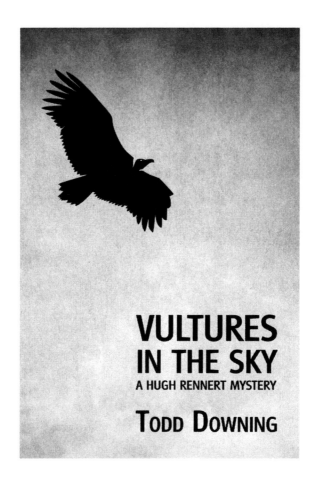

**VULTURES
IN THE SKY**
A HUGH RENNERT MYSTERY

TODD DOWNING

Vultures in the Sky
ISBN 1-61646-149-7

Murder on the Tropic
ISBN 1-61646-150-0

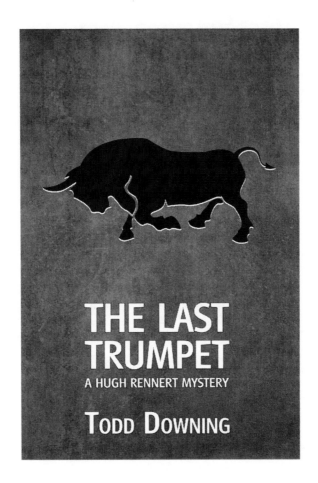

The Last Trumpet
ISBN 1-61646-152-7

Night Over Mexico
ISBN 1-61646-153-5

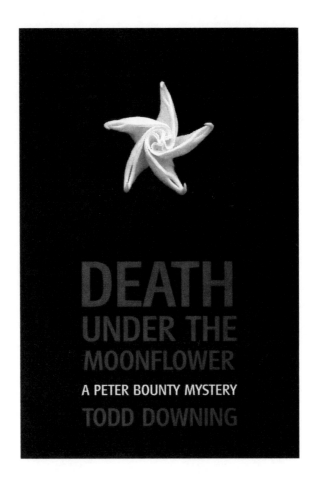

Death under the Moonflower
ISBN 1-61646-157-8

CPSIA information can be obtained at www.ICGtesting.com
Printed in the USA
BVOW07s2141050315

390530BV00006B/311/P